The
Fourth Key

By
Samantha Warren

GET A FREE BOOK!

Get a free copy of one of my books when you sign up for my weekly email of awesomeness. Go here to get your book:

http://www.samantha-warren.com/freebie

CHAPTER ONE

"We've lost Fraeth, Aderwalde and Earchson in the past three days." Boxy tapped a map that sat on the table. It was covered in red, white and black pins that had been stuck into the surface. The white pins, indicating friendly, safe areas, were rapidly being replaced with red pins, indicating combat zones and black pins to show territories that had been lost. The Guardians of the Doors were no longer guardians. They were commanders, leading the armies of Alaesha against the people who threatened to take away their way of life. They were all arranged around the table in the council room of Charles's basement. Veth, Boxy, Edlaner, all of them, including Charles and Edith. This was the very first place Edith had met them all, and it was where she had spent a good portion of her recent time in Alaesha.

Edith sat on the far side of the table and watched the battle-hardened warriors discuss recent events. She had only been in Alaesha a month, but already the war was far larger than she imagined. People Charles knew personally were dying and the few she knew and cared about were constantly put in danger. From the time she found the Third Key, everything in her view of the world had changed. She had discovered a whole new life, a place that had been around longer than the world she previously knew and she had fallen in love with one of the denizens of Alaesha. Charles was valiant, funny and dedicated to his cause. She couldn't help but follow him through the Door to help him keep the Doors safe and protect her own people from being enslaved by the Reformers. But it wasn't what she had expected. She still wasn't sure what that expectation was, but it was far from her current reality.

For a brief moment, she wished she was back home in her crappy little apartment, studying at her tiny little desk for classes at the local community college. Then her nose curled of its own volition and she shook her head. She hated that apartment, and she wouldn't be caught dead at that community college unless it was the only school left on the planet that would accept her.

"Edith?"

She pulled herself from her thoughts and glanced up. The others were staring at her. Her face grew hot and she tried to shrink down into her chair.

"Do you have a problem with our plan?" a tall, wispy woman asked as she crossed her arms. Boxy had been the adviser to the Keeper of the First Key, also known as the Queen of England, before everything went to complete and utter horse poop and the Doors were locked forever. When the Reformers began trying in earnest to steal the keys, and succeeding in some cases, the advisers decided it was best to lock the doors forever and protect the humans from the horrible fate the Reformers were planning for them.

"No," Edith mumbled. "I was just thinking about something else."

Boxy raised an eyebrow. She was clearly unimpressed. "Care to share with us?"

Edith cleared her throat. "No, not really."

The woman snorted. "Please try to pay attention, then. This is important." She gave Edith a hard look before turning back to the map. Edith sank further into the chair and her own shame as her eyes found Charles's. He gave her a small smile. She returned it, but inside, she wanted to scream. She came to Alaesha to do something useful, to help, but so far, all she had done was follow the others around like a puppy and shoot the people they wanted her to shoot. Being just eighteen, she had no experience with weaponry before coming to Alaesha, but Charles discovered

2

she had a special relationship with a magical bow created by her grandfather. The bow listened to her. It felt her. And it did her bidding even if she wasn't a skilled archer. Edith swallowed the bile rising in her throat. Before she met Charles, she had killed exactly zero people. Now the number was pushing twenty.

Her throat burned and dizziness threatened to overtake her. She remembered each and every kill. She wanted to help win a war, but in order to do so, she had become a murderer. The faces of her victims swam in front of her. She pushed herself to her feet and moved toward the door. The conversation stopped and they all looked at her again. "Sorry," she mumbled as she stumbled past a chair. "I just need some air."

Charles came over beside her. He took her arm gently and brushed a lock of dark hair from her forehead. "Are you okay?" The concern on his face melted away the agitation a bit, but the burning in her throat remained.

"Yeah," she said. "I just need to get out of here for a bit. It's too stuffy. It's giving me a headache."

His frown didn't fade as he nodded. He brushed her cheek. "Are you sure you're all right?"

Edith gave him the biggest smile she could muster. "I'm fine, really. I just need some air."

His concern didn't abate, but he gave in. "Okay, but if you go outside, take Ollie. I don't want you wandering around alone."

"I know. I will."

"And take your bow. Always be ready, just in case."

She gave him another, tighter smile. "I will. You've given me this talk before."

His eyebrows knit further together and he took a step back. "I know, I know. I just worry. You're only human and--"

"Charles, we have things to discuss still." Boxy stood at the table with her arms crossed as she stared hard at the pair.

Edith leaned up on her tiptoes and gave Charles a quick kiss. "I'll be fine. Get back to work." With that, she spun on her heel and walked out the door. She closed it behind her and leaned against the wall. Inside, the murmurs continued.

Edith pressed her eyes closed until spots started to form. She took several deep breaths and swallowed to try to clear the bile that was rising up in her throat. It didn't work. She pushed herself away from the wall and headed upstairs. The house still held evidence of the failed rescue attempt the Reformers had made months before. Scorch marks had yet to be painted over. The main hallway was missing much of the decor it had when Edith first arrived. She tried to stay away from the barns where a lot of the destruction had happened. She couldn't bear the thought of seeing the place where innocent creatures were burned to death because some people couldn't get along.

She ran into Mags as she moved toward the stairs. "Edith," Charles's older sister called. Edith spun and found her dusting a painting of their parents that hung along one wall. "What's the matter, dear?"

"Nothing. I just needed some air." Edith tried to give the same excuse she gave to the others, but Mags wasn't having it. While Charles was kind and caring in his own way, Mags was far and away the more empathetic of the pair.

The woman tsked as she walked over. "Nonsense. All the windows are open. It's spring. This house is full of air. What's going on?"

Edith opened her mouth to speak, but Mags held up her hand. "Wait. Meet me on the back patio. I'll be there shortly." She tucked her duster into one of the myriad of pockets on her apron and disappeared through a small door that led to the kitchen.

Edith frowned and considered heading up to her room to lock herself in, which had been her original plan, but her feet had other ideas. They carried her through the house and out onto the back patio where she had eaten dinner her first night in Alaesha. Unlike the indoor garden, which had lost

4

part of its glass ceiling and a good number of its plants to the attack, the back patio was untouched. It looked out over the enormous lawn and the stretch of trees beyond that. It was in those trees where she started to fall for Charles, where he took her to his favorite spot, a gazebo hidden in the woods.

"Here we go," Mags sang as she came out onto the patio. She carried a silver tray stacked with glasses, a pitcher and a plate of tiny sandwiches. "You've been down in that awful room for hours. I figured you must be famished."

Edith gave her a small smile as her stomach rumbled in assent. "Yeah, I guess I'm a little hungry."

"I convinced Niatha to let go of some of that bualdaberry tea you like so much, too." She gave Edith a wink as she set the tray on the wrought iron table and began to pour a glass. "Here you go."

Edith's smile grew as she took the cup. "Thanks, Mags." She took a sip of tea. Bualdaberries were a unique Alaesha berry that tasted like a mash-up of blueberries, grapes and pineapples. Edith had bypassed the bualdaberry muffins when she first arrived, but she had since developed Mags's love for the things. The flavor of the tea exploded onto her tongue, and she closed her eyes to savor the deliciousness for a moment.

Mags poured herself a glass and loaded two small plates with finger sandwiches before settling down across from Edith. "Now, my dear," she said as she picked up a sandwich. "Talk to me."

Edith put her glass down and stared at the plate of sandwiches. There were so many things running through her mind. So many concerns. She was eighteen and she felt like she had the weight of two worlds on her shoulders. And nearly twenty deaths. She missed Dana, the one friend she actually had, and despite the miserable relationship with her mother, she still wanted to see the woman again. Also, part of her wished Charles would forget the war and spend more time with her, but even admitting that to herself made her feel like a petulant child.

"Come now. You're not very good at hiding your feelings, Edith. Even Charles knows something is wrong and he's the most oblivious person I know. Talk to me." Mags leaned forward. "Please."

Edith swallowed as the bile threatened to come up again. "I just..." she began, but she didn't know what she was going to follow it with. She took a deep breath and looked out across the lawn. Ollie, Charles's big horse-sized dog with ears the size of dinner plates, was frolicking with an enchanted stick that would tear off in flight so the big dog could chase it as soon as it was dropped.

Edith tried again. "I'm just not sure I made the right choice. Coming here, I mean." She kept her eyes averted and avoided looking at Mags. She didn't want to see what that normally friendly face might hold.

Mags set her sandwich down. "I see. When did this start?"

Edith shrugged. "A week or two ago, I guess." A grimace crossed her face and she pressed a hand to her chest. "Along with the heartburn."

"Have you talked to Charles about it?"

"No," she said as she shook her head. "He has so much else on his plate, I don't want to bother him."

Mags leaned over. "Edith, you need to talk to Charles. He cares about you deeply. Anything you ask, he'll do."

Edith pressed her lips together. She did believe that, truly. But that childish part of her disagreed. He was absorbed in this war, in protecting her and Alaesha, in making his world a place they could grow old together. She wanted to spend more time with him. She wanted to be able to have this conversation with him, not his sister.

"What are you questioning? Why are you second guessing yourself?" Mags voice held no hint of accusation, just curiosity and concern.

Edith shrugged. "I don't know. I just... It's not what I expected, you know? When I came here, I mean. *Why* I

6

came here. I guess I was just being a foolish child when I left home, thinking going to another world would make everything better, that everything would be fixed."

Mags gave her a small, sad smile. "My dear, no matter where you go or who you're with, nothing will be perfect. That's the way it works. You can't run away from your troubles. There are always good times and bad times."

Edith snorted. "It seems like all we've had are bad times. I feel like I hardly even see Charles anymore unless we are out fighting or talking about fighting. He's always got his head buried in a map or a report or something and I can't get him to talk about anything but the war for more than a minute. It's so frustrating." She pounded a fist on the table and made the plates bounce.

Mags leaned across the table and gripped Edith's hand. "Is that really the problem, Edith? This is war. And like it or not, Charles is one of the best fighters we have."

Tears burned in Edith's eyes. "I know. I know that. Really, I do. And I know in the end, we'll be okay."

"So what's the real problem?"

"All this killing, all this death." She raised her blurry eyes to Mags. "I don't think I can do it anymore. Charles wants me beside him, but it's destroying me. I can't sleep. I have no appetite. All I see are the people I murdered. It's too much."

Mags ran a thumb across the back of Edith's hand. "You need to talk to him, my dear. My brother is very dense, especially when it comes to the female kind. And he tends to have a one-track mind as you've clearly discovered. He needs to know how you're feeling. It's okay if you don't want to do it anymore, but you need to tell him that."

Edith frowned and sighed. "Okay, I'll try to talk to him soon."

Mags patted her hand. "Good girl. Now eat something. You're not a bird." She sipped her tea and gave Edith an I'm-watching-you look.

Edith gave Mags a faint smile. "Yes, ma'am." She picked up a sandwich and took a bite. It was a simple cucumber and butter sandwich, but it was delicious. Niatha truly was an amazing cook, no matter what he laid his hands on. And he didn't need any magic charms to do it. His was pure talent. Edith ate the rest of her sandwiches in the sunshine while Mags prattled on about a new dress she was making for one of Boxy's nieces and tried to forget the ghosts that stood behind her.

CHAPTER TWO

Dana Blake sat at the library, doodling on her homework. Her pretty face was pulled into a permanent frown and her bright blue eyes were dull.

"Dana."

Two weeks into her freshman semester and she was already failing. Dana sighed and doodled some more.

"Dana." The voice was harsher this time. She looked up. The young man across from her raised his eyebrows. "Are you planning on doing some work at any point today? Or am I just wasting your parents money?"

George was her tutor, hired by her parents to help her pass high school and get into college. It worked, but not well. She barely made it into the local community college. They were not impressed. Now George met with her three times a week at the same place she and Edith had studied all summer.

Dana shrugged. "Whatever. I don't care."

"You really should care because this is your future. Do you want to work at a burger joint the rest of your life? Do you enjoy that?"

The young woman's lips puckered as she glanced down at her atrocious red and yellow outfit. It did not suit her at all, and she always smelled of frying oil. "No."

"Then stop moping and get to work." George slapped his hand on the table to emphasize his point, but all it did was earn him a glare from the librarian. "Sorry," he half-whispered as he held up his hand in apology.

Dana rolled her eyes and looked down at her paper. Spanish 102. In high school, she hadn't been great at the language, but she was able to remember enough she could pass the test to skip over Spanish 101. She wished she hadn't. One of the first assignments her professor had given her was to write a five hundred-word essay on her summer break. She sighed.

George scooted around the table so he was almost next to her. His breath smelled like garlic and he leaned in a bit closer than she would have liked. "Here, I can help you. What do you want to say? What did you do this summer?"

Dana looked up at him with a smirk on her lips. "My friend Edith found a key to another world, and we went through the door to join a war. My boyfriend turned out to be from that world and he was a bad guy who tried to kill us all." She gave him a tight smile. "How's that? Do you think you can translate that?"

George frowned. Sometimes he didn't appreciate her sense of humor. "Dana, you need to take this seriously. I don't know what's gotten into you, but you're never going to pass this semester if you don't at least try. Be serious, please."

Dana's smile turned into a sneer. She was being serious, but how could he possibly know that? He was like all the others. Willfully ignorant in their everyday lives, denying the existence of something so much greater than they were. "Yes, sir," she said as she gave him a mocking salute.

George looked at her dubiously, but he pressed on. "Good. Now what did you do this summer?"

Dana spent the rest of the hour making up a completely lame story about going to the beach and buying new clothes. George spent the rest of the hour thinking he had finally gotten through to the younger student and happily helped her translate her summer antics into Spanish.

When the dreadful session was finally over, Dana stuffed her books in her backpack and trudged out the door. It wasn't yet late enough for the sun to be disappearing, so instead of walking toward home, she turned in the other direction. Her parents had taken away her car as punishment for disappearing into Alaesha for over a month without giving them any sort of indication of where she had gone. Her father used the excuse they had to cut back since her stipend for being the Keeper of the Key was no longer coming in, but that stipend would have been halved soon anyway. Her birthday passed almost unmarked three days ago with nothing but a card and a cheap bracelet from her parents. None of her so-called friends even gave her a call. All she got were half-hearted wishes on social media. Lame.

Dana kicked a stone that was in her path. "I miss Edith," she mumbled to no one in particular. The summer hadn't been spectacular, but at least she had had one friend who was there no matter what. They were attached at the hip even though they were nothing alike. Edith was someone she could trust until she disappeared with Charles the night of her eighteenth birthday.

Dana's pout was so deep that she could see her bottom lip. She missed Edith. After the trip into Alaesha where they both nearly died, the girl who was initially her enemy had become her only friend. Edith was the only person she could truly trust, the only one who really seemed to understand her. And Edith now lived on the other side of a door that Dana couldn't go through, helping fight a war that would determine the fate of everyone, and Dana was stuck here in this mundane place, pretending she cared about school, work and all that other stuff that didn't matter in the end.

She plopped herself on the stone wall and looked around. Her wanderings had taken her to a place she had visited many times before. That is, before it burned to the ground. On the outside, however, it just looked like a diner that had been abandoned years before. Alaeshan magic kept the real truth from being revealed. The diner that had once stood there had been leveled with powerful magic into little more than a burned out shell.

Tears blurred Dana's vision as she stared at the diner she had once loved. Some of her best meals had been there.

Charles would often treat her and her family to dinner when he came to visit. Dana's shoulders sank. Her family was still very unhappy with her for losing the key. Not only did they lose the money, but they lost the prestige that came with it, at least as far as Alaeshan circles were concerned. To the normal human world, nothing had changed but Dana's attitude.

Dana sighed and picked up her backpack from where she had dropped it on the ground. She was just about to stand up when a man appeared from around the corner. He was walking quickly and his head was spinning like it was on a swivel as he tried to look every which way at once. Dana ducked behind a nearby tree out of pure instinct. He glanced in her direction, but she remained perfectly still and he didn't see her. She poked her head around the trunk and watched as the man approached the diner.

He kept glancing around as he walked up the steps and tried the door. It jiggled, but didn't give. He peered in a window. From experience, Dana knew he saw nothing but the inside of an abandoned diner. Dusty furnishings, an empty glass, and little else. A charm was in place to encourage people to just keep walking by, and Dana had had to fight the urge with quite a bit of willpower to peer inside. Her distrust of this curious man continued to grow as he tested windows and walked around the building.

Dana left her hiding spot and followed him at a distance. She peered around the corner and watched as he tried the back door. He even picked up a rock and attempted to smash a window, but the rock bounced right off. As he pulled his foot back in an attempt to kick in the back door, Dana tripped over a piece of rubble that had fallen outside the diner.

"Ouch," she hissed just a little too loudly as her toe began to throb.

The stranger froze. His head twisted to the side and his eyes locked on hers. They went wide and he stared at her for the longest ten seconds of her life. Then he turned around so fast that he skidded on the gravel and raced away. Dana tried to follow, but her sandals were not the proper footwear for running. She caught a brief glimpse of him as he disappeared between two buildings, but then he was gone. Dana stared after him for a few minutes. She had no idea what to do. He obviously knew something more than he should and if he was digging around the diner, he could possibly know there was a door in there — a door that no one should have access to.

"Crap," Dana whispered to herself. "Crap, crap, crap." She ran a hand through her blond hair and looked around. "I have to tell someone," she said to herself. "Someone has to know." Her eyes roved around the area for a moment. "Edith's mom," she whispered. She resettled her backpack on her shoulders and took off as fast as her feet could carry her.

The apartment building was as rundown as it had always been. The old woman who had freaked Edith out during her first weeks in the apartment was sitting in her usual spot on the steps. "Hi, Tessa," Dana greeted her as she walked up the cracked sidewalk. "Is Edith's mom home?"

Tessa grinned a toothless grin and bobbed her head. Her clouded eyes found Dana and made the girl feel extremely uncomfortable, but Dana forced herself to take the outstretched hand Tessa offered. The old woman kissed the back of Dana's hand with a sloppy smooch before releasing it. She continued grinning as Dana headed inside.

On the third floor, she found the door to Edith's apartment. She had spent a good part of the summer here when she wasn't at the library with Edith. Her stomach clenched as she knocked. For a moment, she thought no one was home, then the lock slid back. A part of her still expected to see her best friend when the door cracked open, and a tiny piece of her heart broke when it wasn't Edith's face that greeted her.

"Dana? What's wrong?"

Dana opened her mouth, but Edith's mother stopped her. "Wait. You better come in first." She pulled Dana inside and looked down the hall before shutting the door behind her. "Do you want anything to drink?" she asked as she led the way down the short hall.

"No, I'm fine, thank you." A strange feeling settled over Dana as she sank onto the couch. It was in this very spot her life had taken a turn for the worse. "Ms. Myers, I have something I need to tell someone and I don't know who else to tell."

The woman who looked very much like Edith narrowed her eyes at Dana. "Okay, go ahead."

Dana took a deep breath and told Edith's mother all about the man at the diner. She was done quickly and felt foolish for being concerned about a man who was poking around in an old diner. "I'm sorry," she said as she finished. "It's probably nothing. I shouldn't be bugging you with it."

Ms. Myers took her hand. "No, you were right to come tell me. There have been rumors of attempts to break through the doors from this side. And with the Third Door unguarded as it is, there is great risk. Did the man look human? Or was he Alaeshan?"

Dana snorted. "You're asking me? Don't forget, I'm a horrible judge of character." Dana's ex-boyfriend had been an Alaeshan in disguise who was trying to steal the key from her when she was the Keeper. That was just another thing her parents were upset about, even though she had dated him for four months and they were none the wiser, either.

Edith's mom gave her a small smile and patted her cheek. "We all make mistakes, dear. Trust me."

Dana frowned. "I seem to be making a lot of them lately."

Edith's mom snorted. "That's the way it tends to work. One day, you're on top the of the world. The next, you're at the bottom of a trash pile." She straightened and put a determined look on her face. "But now is not the time for moping. We need to figure out who this guy is and what he wants. Will you help me?"

Dana felt her face pull into a grin at the idea of being needed again. "Absolutely, Ms. Myers. I'd love to."

14

"Excellent. But from now on, you call me Elva, okay? No more of this Ms. Myers stuff. That was my mother." The woman patted Dana's hand.

"Yes, ma'am. Elva." For the first time in a long time, Dana was excited.

CHAPTER THREE

A knock on the door startled Edith from her musings. She slid her feet off the window seat and walked over to answer it. As she cracked it open, she saw dark curly hair surrounding a grinning face.

"Mags said you wanted to see me."

Edith silently cursed the woman. She hadn't intended on actually talking to Charles about anything that wasn't absolutely necessary. Now she had no choice.

"Yeah, come in." She stepped aside so he could enter the room.

He leaned over and gave her a kiss on the cheek as he walked past. She gave him a tight smile and bowed her head.

His eyes narrowed. "Everything okay?"

She half shrugged a single shoulder. "Sort of. Have a seat." She waved a hand at the window.

He settled onto the bench and she sat next to him with one leg folded underneath her. Sitting that way served two purposes. First, it turned her so she could see out the window and avoid looking directly at Charles. Second, it put a little distance between them so she wasn't sitting right next to him.

"So what's up?" Charles leaned back against the wall.

Edith stared out the window. The sun was setting and a light breeze tickled the leaves of the trees nearby. She searched for the right words, the way to start a hard, uncomfortable conversation. Language failed her.

"Edith?" Charles reached over and laid a hand on her knee. It still made tingles run up her spine when he touched her, but a part of her cringed.

She took a deep breath and released it. "Um," she began, still unsure of what exactly she wanted to say. "Well..." She sighed in frustration. "I don't know how to put it. Not really. I mean, I know what I want to say, I just don't know how to say it. Does that make any sense at all?" She sighed again and leaned her head against the window.

Charles squeezed her knee gently. "Edith, just tell me. If I don't know what's going on, I can't help fix it."

Edith watched as the last sliver of sun disappeared below the tree line. She felt like she was sinking with it. She pressed her fingertips to the window and imagined what would happen if she suddenly just fell through. "Why am I here?" she whispered.

"What? What do you mean?" Charles gentle squeeze turned into a gentle grip.

Edith blinked away the stinging tears that were forming in her eyes and sat up a little straighter. She fixed her eyes on Charles. "Why am I here? What is my purpose in Alaesha? All I seem to do is kill people. Is that why you brought me here? To be a killing machine? I'm not even very good at it. Boxy, Veth—all them are ten times better than me. I just pick off the people on the edges." She leaned forward. "Why am I here, Charles?"

His mouth worked like a fish and for a moment, Edith felt terrible at putting him on the spot like that. Then he spoke. "You came to be with me, didn't you?"

Edith couldn't stifle the short, hard laugh that bubbled in her throat. "Yeah, I did, but the only time we're actually together is when we're out killing people or talking about killing people. Do you even realize that? Have you even noticed that we never see each other anymore? Or are you so caught up in this war, it's the only thing that matters to you? Do you even care about me at all?" All the anger and sadness that had been simmering in Edith's gut boiled over. Her body hummed with it and her throat burned with bile.

Pink rose to her cheeks as she realized how utterly ridiculous she sounded. The world was in a war. She was there to help. And yet she felt like a toddler having a temper tantrum. What was wrong with her?

Charles stared at her. His eyes were as wide as Ollie's ears. "I had no idea you felt like that," he mumbled as he lowered his head.

Edith snorted despite herself. Inside, she was screaming at herself to shut up, but her mouth kept moving. "No, of course you didn't. You have one focus. Anything outside that just doesn't matter."

When Charles looked up again, the hurt on his face was as plain as an open, bleeding wound. "That's not fair," he whispered.

Edith glanced away out the window, but the anger inside began to ebb as the guilt at attacking him began to take over. He was right. It wasn't fair, and she was being childish, but she refused to admit that out loud.

"Edith, this war is huge. You only just got here, so you don't understand it all yet, but this is literally a battle to the death. This will decide the fate of my world and yours." He leaned forward and put his hand on her knee again. "I love you, Edith. I do. Very much so. And I'm sorry if you haven't felt that. I didn't just bring you here to kill people." His lips pulled into a half smile. "You're right. You're not very good at it. But it strengthens me to have you by my side. To know you're there through it all."

A surge of electricity raced across Edith's skin. He loved her? That single thought raced through her mind, over and over. He loved her. He really, truly loved her and despite all the time he spent on the war, he wanted to be with her. Only her. Her heart began to melt. She looked up at Charles. The sincerity on his face was almost more than she could bear. She bit her lip. In that moment, she could almost forget about the war. "You love me?"

His smile grew and he cupped her cheek. "Yes. I do. This war, all this fighting, I do it for you. For our future. For our children."

Edith sat back a little bit. She was eighteen and they were soldiers in the middle of a major crisis. Children were the absolute last thing on her mind. She wasn't even sure she wanted them. And here he was, discussing their future like it was an absolute certainty. She held up her hands. "Whoa now. You're jumping the gun a bit there, aren't you?"

He grinned. "Maybe a little. But I want a life with you, Edith. I want us to raise a family in a world that isn't torn by war. Don't you want the same thing?"

She inhaled and lowered her eyes. "Yes, I do. Someday."

"Then this is what we have to do to make that happen. We have to fight for what we want. This war isn't going to end on its own. And even though I don't like it, I'm a big part of it." He shrugged a shoulder. "That's just who I am. My family has always played a leading role in the way Alaesha is run. I can't change that."

Edith's shoulders sank and she stared at her hands until Charles reached over to take one.

"Is that the only thing bothering you?"

Yes sat on her lips, but after a brief pause, she shook her head.

"Tell me." He reached out and pulled her close.

She leaned into him. Part of her was afraid to admit the truth, afraid of his reaction. But a bigger part of her wanted him to know, to tell her it was okay and she would never have to do it again. "I don't want to kill anyone anymore."

He sat back. "But Edith, that's what war is. That's the only way we'll win."

She ran a hand through her hair. Her heart pounded and the bile ate at the back of her tongue. All the faces of those she had killed flashed before her eyes. "I know," she said. "But I hate it. I hate it so much." She raised her eyes to Charles's. "Please don't make me do it anymore."

The area between his eyebrows puckered in concern. He cupped her cheek. "We need your help with this one battle, and then I promise, no more." He leaned forward and kissed her nose. "I wish you would have told me you felt this way sooner. We could have avoided a lot of stress for you. If things start to get to you like this again, please tell me. I can read your mind if I have to, but I really don't want to."

She glanced up at him. He was smiling. She inhaled deeply and nodded. "Okay. I will. If I start to feel like this again, I'll tell you." In her mind, she completed the sentence. *Maybe.*

He squeezed her hand. "Good. I hate when you're upset. It makes it hard for me to focus on other things."

Edith's smile faded from her face.

Charles patted her knee. "Everything's going to be all right in the end. I promise. We're doing well and the Reformers have been pushed back. They still have the Seventh Door and have surrounded the Fourth, but that won't last. We have a plan for bringing them to their knees. That's what we were working on today. Someday soon, Alaesha will be free of this war, and then we can really start our life together, the right way."

His smile was so big and so hopeful, Edith didn't want to destroy it. "Great," she said. "The sooner the better."

He leaned over and gave her a quick peck on the cheek. "I'm glad we talked. I knew something was bothering you, but I didn't know what. This war is hard on everyone and you're not used to the way things are done here. It'll all sort itself in the end. I promise." He gave her another smile. "But now, I need to get going. Boxy and Nach are waiting downstairs. We're still hashing out that plan. We're going to eat dinner and keep working." He stood up. "Want to join us?"

Edith gave him a small smile. "No thanks. I think I'll just have Niatha send something up. I'm feeling a bit tired."

"Okay. Get some sleep." He kissed her on the top of her head and gave her a wink before leaving.

Edith waited until the door shut before she let the tears flood her eyes. They stung, but she didn't fight them. All the frustration she felt bubbled to the surface and boiled over in the salty drops running down her cheeks. She let them flow, hoping they would cleanse her of the awful feelings burning in her gut.

She hadn't told Charles the real truth, only part of it. She wanted to, but couldn't. She stared out the window as the rest of the light disappeared and tried to wish herself home, back to that crappy apartment, back to her mother and Dana, where she knew what life held for her and didn't have to kill anyone or worry that her boyfriend wouldn't make it through the next battle.

CHAPTER FOUR

"Let's start with a simple one," George said as he tapped the textbook that lay open on the table. "Here. Look at problem number fifteen. It's not hard. If a>0 and b>0, which of the following could be an equation of the line graphed in the xy-plane?"

Dana blinked as she started at the page. "Um, c?"

George sighed. "You're just guessing. Again."

Dana shrugged. "Yeah, but am I right?"

Her tutor gave her a small smirk. "Yes. You have an uncanny knack for guessing the right answer even if you have no idea what it is."

"It works."

George shook his head. "It won't work forever." He leaned forward across the table. "Dana, you're eighteen years old. You have no marketable skills. Cheerleader isn't exactly a big selling point on a resume."

Dana glared at him. "Algebra won't exactly get me anywhere either. Who actually uses this crap?"

George straightened his shoulders. "I do. I use it almost every day."

"Because you're still in college, like me. Just because you're a senior, it doesn't mean you're any further along than I am. Not really. Neither of us are anything. We're just worthless humans walking along in a lie, pretending to be something we're not."

George stared at her. His mouth worked as he tried to comprehend what was going on.

"Forget it," Dana said as she rose from the table. "I have to go." She began stuffing her books into her bag.

"Dana, you really need to study this."

"I'll study later." She threw her bag over her shoulder. "Bye, George."

She was already halfway to the door when he said, "Bye, I guess."

Dana stopped on the steps and looked around. To the left and about five blocks down was home. To the right lay the Third Door. She walked down to the sidewalk and turned right. Half an hour later, she found herself back in front of the diner. She set her bag on the ground next to the steps and looked up at the door. The glass was dusty as if it had been years since anyone had been there instead of just a few months ago.

She walked up the steps and ran her finger over the window. She expected it to come away covered in dirt, but it didn't. Only a thin layer of city dust coated her skin. The line wasn't even visible in the image projected on the window. She gripped the door handle and tried to open the door. It rattled, but didn't budge. She put her shoulder against the frame and pushed. A faint hum came from inside the diner. She pushed harder. The hum grew and she found herself thrown back from the door. She stumbled to the edge of the stairs and leaned against the railing.

"Ow," she said aloud as she rubbed her shoulder. The jolt of electricity was still buzzing through her arm. It wasn't enough to hurt her, but it was enough to deter her from trying again. "Not cool." She glared at the door for a moment before trudging back down the stairs. She picked up her pack and walked across the street to settle on the stone wall she sat on the day before.

It wasn't long before someone came walking down the street. Dana stayed where she was, out in the open, clearly visible, and watched. Sure enough, it was the same man who had been trying to get in the diner the day before. He glanced around. His eyes flitted across her. For a brief moment, their eyes locked, then he turned away and disappeared behind the diner.

"He saw me," Dana said to herself. A frown crept across her face. He knew she was there. It was almost as if he expected to see her. She picked up her bag and followed him around the corner of the diner.

His black shirt was just disappearing into the alcove for the back door when Dana came around the corner. She stood there, unsure of what to do. She was following a strange man who obviously wanted her to follow him, someone who was trying to break into a magical diner that protected a door into another world.

She glanced around the area. There wasn't a single other person in sight. "This is really dumb," Dana mumbled. She tucked her bag beside the steps and felt along her arm. She pulled back a skin-colored piece of fabric and removed the thin knife that lay against her forearm. She gripped it in her hand and crept up the stairs.

The door was already open, beckoning her inside. She squeezed her knife tighter and held it out in front of her as she walked into the abandoned diner. Dana peered into the murkiness. The inside of the diner looked much different than the outside. One wall was almost completely gone. Light streamed in and illuminated the area. Cans littered the floor. All the shelves were knocked over, blocking the aisles and creating haphazard, dangerous arches.

A metallic clank sounded from over by the entrance to the stairs that led down to the Third Door. Dana's fingers turned white as her knife led the way. She ducked under an upside-down V created by two warped metal shelves, and there he was.

A gun pointed at Dana's head as she straightened on the other side of the arch. "Drop the knife."

The big black hole of the muzzle filled her vision. Her breath seized in her chest. She pictured the bullet flying out, reaching her before she had a chance to react, burying itself in her forehead. Her body would fall and lay there, possibly forever. Her parents would have no idea where she was, but they might just figure she ran away. It wasn't the first time she would have disappeared without warning. Her fingers released of their own accord and the only weapon she had clattered to the ground.

The man jerked his head to the side. "Move over there. Slowly."

Dana glanced to where he indicated. It was a small space between the fallen shelves and the wall. There were no other paths and no way out except through him.

"Hurry up," he commanded as he waved his gun to the corner. "Move it."

Dana's heart thudded in her chest and her blood roared through her ears. A lump formed in her throat and made it hard to swallow. Her whole body shook, but she did what she was told and scurried over to the corner with her hands still up.

"Who are you? Why are you following me?" The man's bright eyes narrowed at her. His mouth pulled into a tight line.

I'm going to die here, she thought to herself. *And no one is going to know.* Her hands shook and her skin paled.

"I..." Her voice cracked. Her skin felt like it was crawling over her bones and her head swam. "I'm..." Breathing was impossible. Her chest clenched.

The man stared at her for a moment. Then he lowered his gun. "Aww, crap. I'm sorry." He tucked his gun into the back of his jeans and moved over beside her. "Are you okay?"

"Can't... breathe." Just those two words took all of Dana's willpower. She pressed her hand to her chest and prayed for the pain to stop. She was only eighteen. That was much too young to have a heart attack, but she couldn't think of any other reason for her heart to be pounding the way it was.

He patted her on the back. "You're having a panic attack. Put your hands on your knees. Just focus on inhaling and exhaling. Just breathe."

Dana's eyelids fluttered as she tried to clear her vision. The man kept talking in a low, soft voice and she followed his instructions. After several terrifying minutes, her chest relaxed, her heart slowed, and she no longer felt like she was dying.

"Good, good," the man said. "Here, sit down for a minute." He tucked his hand under her elbow and helped her settle on the dust-covered floor. "Are you feeling better?"

Dana nodded. "A little."

The man sank down onto his haunches in front of her. "I'm really sorry about that. I'm not very good at this whole thing."

Dana eyed him. "What whole thing?" she asked. "Who are you?"

He looked at her a moment while he chewed his lip. "I guess I owe you that much. My name is Aidan." He held out his hand.

She looked at it a moment before taking it. His hands were warm, but rough as if he used them quite often. She didn't offer her own name in return. "Thank you," she said instead. "For helping with that." She waved her hand to indicate the panic attack.

"It was nothing. My sister has them all the time. You get them a lot?"

Dana shook her head. "No. This was the first. It felt like I was dying."

He nodded as his face pinched in concern. "Yeah, that's what she says. I've never had one, so I can't really relate, but I really am sorry for scaring you so bad. I've never been very good at confronting people."

"Why are you breaking into the diner?"

He shrugged. "Something to do?"

Dana frowned at him. "That's not an answer."

"It's a complicated story. You'd probably think I was crazy if I told you the truth."

"I can believe quite a lot. Why don't you give it a try?"

26

He settled on the floor next to her. "All right. There's a hidden door underneath this diner that leads to another world and I want to get through it."

Dana didn't know what her face showed, but the man's eyes lit up. "You already know about the door," he mused. "That's why you were here. You were looking for a way in."

She had no idea why, but she felt comfortable around him. Still, she didn't directly answer his question. She wasn't even sure of it herself. Did she want to go in? Was she protecting the door? She didn't know yet. Instead, she said, "My best friend is on the other side."

"Your best friend?" He squinted at her and examined her face a bit closer. Recognition dawned on him after a moment. "You're Dana," he exclaimed. "The old Keeper!"

She blushed and lowered her head. "Yeah, well…"

He picked up her hand and shook it again. "It's such a pleasure to meet you. I've never met a bonafide Keeper before. This is so crazy. I can't believe I didn't recognize you. I'm so sorry. I should have. I feel like such an idiot."

Dana gave him a quick, faint smile and extracted her hand from his. "Why do you want to get through? Are you Alaeshan?"

Aidan shifted uncomfortably. "No, not exactly."

Dana raised an eyebrow. "Then what exactly? A Reformer?" Her shoulders tensed and she glanced around for her knife.

"No," he said as he raised his hands and patted the air. "Nothing like that. Well, sort of. It's really very complicated."

"I've got time." Dana fluttered between trusting him and wanting to kill him. For some strange reason, her gut told her she could believe him, but she knew nothing about him. She found herself trusting her instinct and trusting him.

He leaned back. "Okay, well, I don't. That's why I'm kind of glad I met you."

"You're glad you met me? Why's that?"

He smiled. "Because I need your help."

27

CHAPTER FIVE

"Thanks, Mags." Boxy picked up a glass of wine and sipped it as Mags finished setting dinner on the table. The other woman bobbed her head once and picked up the empty tray before disappearing into the house. "She's been quiet lately," Boxy remarked after she was gone.

Charles looked up from the bread he was picking apart. "Has she? I hadn't noticed."

Boxy gave him a wry smile and sipped her wine again.

Edith stared at the food in front of her. It looked delicious as Niatha's food always did, but her appetite wasn't what it used to be. She didn't particularly want to be sitting on the patio with Charles and Boxy as they discussed the latest battle plans, but she didn't feel like she had a choice in the matter. Charles had asked that she join them so nicely. How could she say no?

"The best plan of attack is to surround the camp completely," Boxy was saying. "Give them no chance of escape."

Charles stuffed a forkful of orange pasta into his mouth and shook his head. He chewed it before disagreeing with Boxy. "No. He's smart. Probably has a few escape routes already planned just in case. We need a distraction. We need to make him think he's safe when he's not."

Edith poked at the food on her plate. Listening to the talk around her made her stomach churn. The taste of bile rose to her mouth. She couldn't remember why she had enjoyed it when she first came to Alaesha.

"Edith," Boxy said from across the table. "What do you think?"

The younger woman looked up. Boxy's white hair floated around her head as a light breeze blew across the patio. Both she and Charles were staring at Edith, awaiting her response.

"Um, well," Edith began as she moved food around on her plate. She shifted in her seat and wished she could crawl out of her skin.

"Well?" Boxy prompted.

Edith shrugged. "I don't know. I guess it depends on who he is. Why are we attacking the camp? What's the purpose? What are we trying to accomplish?"

Boxy looked at her with wide, baffled eyes for a moment, then she turned to Charles. "Do you tell the girl nothing?"

Charles blushed and shrugged. "I thought she knew."

Edith imagined herself telling Boxy, "No, he doesn't tell me a damn thing and it's starting to piss me off," but she kept her lips pressed firmly together.

Boxy took another sip of wine. "His name is Gereld Anar. He is a scientist." She said the word like it was the most vile thing she could imagine.

Edith frowned. "A scientist?"

"Yes." Boxy's nose curled. "A scientist."

Edith raised her eyebrows at Charles. "Why is that a bad thing? What has he done?"

Both Charles and Boxy stared at Edith until she shifted in her seat.

"What?" she asked with a bit more fire in her voice than she intended.

Boxy shook her head at Charles. "You weren't kidding. She really does know nothing. Maybe this isn't the best place for her. Maybe she should go back to her own world. It would be safer for her there, for a time at least. She does not have the knowledge or resolve she needs to be a part of this war."

29

"No," Charles insisted. "She needs to be here. She has talent and the bow responds to her. She's a part of this. She helped us get this far. She deserves to see it go all the way."

Edith was torn. Charles was defending her, protecting her. She should be grateful, but part of her agreed with Boxy. She really didn't know much about this war. She knew what Charles told her and she had encountered some pretty terrible Reformers, but nothing is ever as simple as black and white in war and politics.

Boxy rolled her eyes and sighed, but she said, "Fine. But I don't like it." She turned to Edith. "Gereld is a scientist. Here, in Alaesha, scientists are not heralded as heroes. They don't cure cancer. They don't build bombs."

"How are bombs a good thing?" Edith asked.

Boxy narrowed her eyes. "Magic scientists are powerful, horrible people, Edith. They play with magic. They try to dissect it, to change it, to control it in a way beyond the norm. They are immoral, illogical and evil. Magic science is an abomination. Magic is just that: magic. It is mysterious and wonderful. It should not be questioned or experimented on. It is sacred."

The longer Boxy spoke, the more powerful her voice got. It pressed on Edith and she sank back into her chair until Boxy finally finished.

"Has he built something dangerous?" Edith finally asked.

Charles shook his head. "No, Edith. It's much worse. He has used his knowledge to find a way through the doors. Without the keys. He can enter your world at any time and no one can stop him."

Edith stared at her hands. They were shaking. She thought of her mother and Dana on the other side of the door. She knew where the Third Door was. It was safe. But what about the others? Who was guarding them? "You have all the doors protected, right? All except the Seventh? No one can get through them, can they? Not without a fight. You told me no one could get through. You told me the doors knew not to let the bad guys through."

Boxy's mouth pressed into a hard line. It was Charles who answered her question. "When magic science comes into play, nothing is safe. Nothing is sacred. Scientists have no concern for others. They care for no one but themselves. They only want destruction. That's what they live for. The Reformers want to enslave your people and destroy your world as they've tried to destroy ours. The scientists want to help them do that."

"So why don't we just destroy the camp, then? We have those bombs Boxy talked about the other day. The ones that will destroy anything in a couple miles. Why not take up a carriage and drop one on the camp? Just take it out completely? Then you wouldn't have to worry about the scientist anymore."

Charles glanced at Boxy. The hard lines at the corners of her eyes did not disappear. "We can't do that," she said. "We need him alive."

Edith's mouth opened and closed several times before a single word formed on her tongue. "Why?"

"Why? Because he is still a very powerful magician. If we can convince him to join us, we can use his talents for good."

"But..." Edith's mind couldn't wrap around the questions she wanted to ask, the contradictions that were blatantly laying on the table with the food.

Charles leaned over and patted her hand. "I know. It's hard to understand. Alaesha is a complicated world, much more complicated than yours." He smiled at her. "You'll get it one day."

She returned his smile, but it was forced. As Boxy and Charles began discussing other plans again, Edith leaned back in her chair and stared at the table. *No*, she thought. *I get it. He's only evil if he's not on your side.* The others seemed so oblivious to that fact. Did they not realize how two-faced they were being? She glanced up at the two people she had trusted so completely and wondered once again if moving to Alaesha and trusting people she really barely knew was a smart decision.

CHAPTER SIX

"Hurry," Charles whispered into the darkness. "Over here."

Edith bent low and kept her head behind the bushes as she followed him through the night. They circled around the Reformer encampment while Boxy and the rest of their attack squad went the other way.

"He's up there." Charles knelt down and pointed.

Edith's gaze followed his finger. Sure enough, a man sat on a branch high up in a tree. He had a large looking glass plastered to his eye as he kept watch over the camp. It wasn't a large camp, but they were dangerous, nonetheless.

"Take him," Charles mumbled in her ear.

She grabbed an arrow from her quiver and placed it in the Gathle crossbow she loved so much. She had used it daily since coming back to Alaesha and it felt a part of her, an extension of her flesh. She was beginning to understand why. Certain weapons were created with more than just tools. Some were created with a magic more powerful than anything that could be seen. William Gathle, the creator of the bow, was her grandfather. His blood flowed through her veins and the bow reacted to that. The bow recognized her as worthy of its obedience and did its best to please her.

Edith knelt beside Charles and raised the bow. She sighted along the top, searching the trees until she found the man. He was looking out over the camp, scanning for anyone who might try to invade them while the rest of them were sleeping. She waited while he turned in her direction.

She and Charles were hidden from those in the camp, but not from him. His looking glass locked on them.

His eye found Edith. It saw her bow pointed in his direction. His mouth opened to call a warning, but in the same instant he drew breath, she let the arrow fly. It soared through the air, brushing aside leaves on its way to its target.

The man leaned back as if doing so would save him, but he kept the looking glass pressed to his eye. All the better to watch his doom approach, Edith though. The arrow hit the glass with a pop and slid through the tube until it connected with the man's face.

He jerked back, but it was too late. His head slammed into the tree and he slid from his perch. Charles raced forward to grab him before he hit the ground, but he didn't need to. The man lodged in the crook of the tree just below the branch he had been sitting on. The looking glass dangled from his head, held in place by the arrow and its feathers.

Edith's nose curled and she swallowed hard to keep her lunch from making an appearance.

Charles slipped an arm around her and pulled her close enough to kiss her hair. "Nice aim, love. You're getting good at this."

Edith gave him a little smile, but inside her stomach was on fire. She had become a killer once more, and she didn't much like it—in fact, she hated it.

Charles tilted his head and pressed a button on his shoulder. "Boxy, it's a go. Repeat, it's a go."

Two clicks came back over the little speakers they both wore in their ears. Charles bobbed his head forward. While the main assault was happening on the other side of the camp, Charles and Edith had another job to do. They slipped through the bushes until they found the tent they were looking for. It was gray, just like all the rest, but it was about twice the size and surrounded by smaller ones.

Charles squatted beside one of the smaller tents and waited. A knife was in his hand and it glittered in the pale light of the quarter moon. Edith reloaded her bow. She found herself stroking the wood with her thumb. She didn't stop herself from doing it. It comforted her.

A shout went up from across the camp. Charles tensed. A scream followed the shout. The sounds doubled, then tripled. Soon, the whole camp was awake and surging toward the attackers on the other side of the small field.

On the other side of the fabric, a woman shouted in a language Edith was still trying to learn. The only word she caught was "death." She glanced at Charles. He winked at her. Despite his claims to the opposite, he always seemed more alive in times like this, just before the battle started. He seemed to look forward to the chaos that was soon to erupt. Edith wasn't sure how she felt about that, but she pushed the thought aside to deal with another time. It wasn't the first time she had noticed it, and it wouldn't be the last. She would deal with it someday, but not today.

The woman's shouts faded away as she ran to join the fight. "Let's go," Charles whispered. He stood up into a crouch and crept around the small tent.

Edith followed. Across the camp, the battle was clearly in full swing. A handful of tents burned on the edges and screams were more frequent. The sound of sword clanging against sword echoed through the night sky and spurts of magic in all its various forms could be seen through the gaps.

"Over here," Charles said as he ran toward the big tent. He paused at the wide, flat back and raised his knife. It was a beautiful knife, Edith had to admit. While the hilt was simple leather, the blade itself was a sight to behold. It looked as if it had been inlaid with thousands of tiny diamonds, but Charles told her it was just the metal that was used and the magic it was imbued with. It was a rare, insanely expensive blend that one of the most famous weaponsmiths had come up with. No one had been able to duplicate it, so the weapons he created were beyond valuable.

The knife had been a gift to Charles's mother. Now it sank into the fabric of the tent with ease. Charles pulled it down and made a wide slit. He poked his head inside a moment before slipping through. Edith nocked an arrow in her bow and followed.

A man stood near the doorway to the tent. He was tall and stick-thin, bare-chested with the same ebony skin that Alex had had after he turned. His white hair was long and bound back into a ponytail. He held the flap aside as he looked out into the night. A sword dangled in his left hand with its point touching the ground.

Charles slipped up to the man as quiet as a mouse sneaking around a cat. In one swift motion, he grabbed the man's sword arm and jerked him back. He pressed his body against the man's taller form and laid the blade against his throat.

"Don't move," he growled into the man's ear. The man stiffened against him, but did as he was told.

As all this was happening, Edith scanned the room with her bow. The interior of the tent was dark. The thick fabric kept out the light of the torches, but it couldn't stop the screams and shouts that were growing ever closer.

"What do you want?" the man hissed.

"You," Charles said. "Gereld Anar, I am hereby declaring you a prisoner of the Alaeshan army."

A whimper burst into the tent from a corner hidden by darkness. Edith spun toward it with her bow raised. At the same time, Charles turned his head. Gereld threw his own head back and smashed his skull into Charles's cheek bone. Charles reeled back. The knife fell from the man's throat, but not before leaving a gash. It wasn't fatal, but the blood flowed freely.

The man raised his sword and pointed it at Charles. His smile was tight. "No, Charles Korwel. I'm declaring *you* a prisoner of the Reformer army." He took a step forward. "And oh, what a prize you are."

Charles had his hands out and the knife was pointed up. It balanced between his thumb and the lower part of his forefinger. The other fingers were pointed out.

"Drop the knife," Gereld demanded as he took another step forward.

"Or what?" Charles raised his chin and looked the man in the eye. "You know you can't take me in a fair fight."

Gereld sneered. "We're not going to fight. You and your human wench are going to surrender. You can't break our defenses."

Edith kept her bow pointed toward the corner as she glanced out the door. The sounds of battle were growing closer and more tent fires were visible.

"I think we already have," she said. Another whimper came from the corner. She spun back and raised her bow higher. As she took a step forward, so did Gereld.

He moved toward Charles and raised his sword. Charles had just enough time to bring his knife up. The blade of the sword skittered along the shorter blade of the glittering knife and slid away harmlessly. Charles stepped in. The maneuverability of the knife gave him more room to work than the long sword gave Gereld. He slashed at the Reformer's left arm, severing the muscles in the forearm. The man screamed and dropped the sword. He dropped to his knees and pressed his hand against the wound.

"Papa!" The whimper in the corner turned to a scream. A small body leapt up from behind a chest.

Edith's touchy finger smacked the release on the bow, but she jerked it as she did and the arrow went wide.

"Jilda!" Gereld shouted and rose to his feet. He slammed his shoulder into Charles's stomach and drove the other man back.

Edith grabbed another arrow and slammed it into the bow. The Reformer tackled Charles to the ground and raised his right fist. He smashed it into Charles's face. Once, twice. He drew back for another punch.

Edith let the arrow fly. It sank into Gereld's side. He grunted and tumbled off to the side.

"Papa," Jilda cried as she ran the last few steps to her father. She sank down beside him as sobs wracked her little body. "Papa," she whispered. She threw herself over him and covered his chest as best she could.

Gereld brought up his right arm and wrapped it around the little girl. "Jilda," he said as he pressed his forehead to hers.

Edith nocked the bow and walked over. She held it pointed at the pair, but her heart was racing. Everyone she had killed so far had been an adult. Now she had her bow pointed at a little girl, a child, someone who had no part in the war aside from being the daughter of a man the Alaeshans wanted to kill. Did she have what it would take to make that kill? She didn't think so. She hoped she didn't.

Edith's lips pressed into a tight line. The acid in her stomach was a hurricane of chaos and the bile was rising into her throat. She swallowed, but all she could taste was the coppery stench of blood. Her bow lowered until the arrow pointed toward the ground at Gereld's feet.

Charles climbed to his feet. He retrieved the knife and walked over to Gereld. The little girl was splayed across her father's body and couldn't see as Charles pointed the blade at her head.

Edith wanted to protest. She wanted to tell Charles to drop the knife, or at least move it away from the little girl, but voice failed her. Was Charles the type of man who would kill a child? She didn't know. She didn't want to find out.

"Surrender," Charles said. His voice was calm and even, almost sad.

Gereld held his daughter tight and pressed his lips to her forehead for a moment. "I surrender," he said.

Charles nodded and held out his free hand. Edith put her bow aside and knelt down to help the little girl up. Jilda fought as her hands touched her.

"It's all right," Gereld soothed. "They won't hurt us."

Gereld's eyes met Edith's in a silent plea to prove him right. She nodded her head. "That's right. We're not going to hurt you. I promise."

37

She glanced up at Charles. His eyes narrowed a bit, but he kept his mouth shut.

Edith helped the little girl to her feet. Then Gereld took Charles's hand. It was an odd moment, watching the Alaeshan help a Reformer, but the moment was broken as soon as Gereld was on his feet. Charles spun him around and bound the man's hands behind his back, ignoring the pained groans coming from the Reformer as Charles jerked on his injured arm.

The little girl whimpered as she watched her father being manhandled.

"Charles," Edith said through clenched teeth.

When he glanced at her, she widened her eyes and bobbed her head toward Jilda. He shrugged and shook his head. Edith did it again.

"I don't know what you're asking." Irritation tinged the edge of his voice.

Edith fought the urge to roll her eyes. "Would you want to watch your father being jerked about by the bad guys? Be a little nicer, please."

Charles's lips puckered, but he stopped jerking Gereld around as he finished binding his hands.

Edith knelt in front of the little girl. "Where's your mother?"

Jilda pointed at the door of the tent. "Out there."

"She's fighting?"

The little girl nodded. "She's papa's guardian."

"Bloody good job, eh?" Charles grinned and tossed Edith a wink. She returned it with a glare. Charles sighed and grabbed the rope tied to Gereld's hands. "Let's go."

He pushed the man toward the hole in the back of the tent and held the point of the glittery knife to his throat. "Don't try anything," he demanded.

"You have a knife to my throat and you have my daughter. I am yours to command." Gereld sounded defeated and Edith believed him completely. He would do anything to protect his child. He may be a Reformer, but he was a father first. She admired him for that and mentally vowed to do everything in her power to protect his child as long as he was in Charles' custody.

She picked up the little girl and balanced her on one hip with the bow in her other hand. "How old are you, Jilda?"

Jilda pressed her lips together and looked at her father. He nodded. "Four," she said.

"Four? You're getting so big!"

The little girl's lips twitched in a quick smile at the compliment.

Edith pressed on. "Do you have anything you want to take with you, like a dolly or blanky?"

Charles raised his eyebrows at Edith. "Dolly? Blanky? It's like I don't even know you anymore."

She narrowed her eyes at Charles. He may have been joking, but he was right. In reality, they had only known each other for a few months and all of them had been during a war. They had never had a date. He knew very little about her past, or the fact that she babysat her next door neighbor's daughter all summer when she was sixteen. "You really don't," she said as she brushed a chunk of hair from Jilda's face.

He blinked at her as she set the little girl down and took her hand. Jilda led her over to the corner where she had been hiding and picked up a small doll. It was dirty and torn, but it looked well-loved. She held it close as Edith led her to the rip in the back of the tent.

"One second," Edith said. She dropped the little girl's hand and fitted an arrow onto the bow. It was heavy to carry one-handed and she had to prop it against her hip to hold it up, but she wasn't about to let the little girl run off. She reached over and gripped Jilda's hand tightly. "Stay with me, okay? I'll keep you safe."

Jilda's eyes were wide as saucers, but she nodded and pressed herself close to Edith.

Edith slipped through the hole in the tent and scanned her bow back and forth. It was still quiet on this side of the camp. All the fighting remained on the far side, near the entrance. She led the way through the trees with Jilda just behind her. Charles pushed Gereld along in front of him and kept an eye out behind them.

They were almost back to the agreed-upon meeting spot when a shout echoed from Edith's right. She spun and raised her bow as a figure broke from the trees. It barreled toward them with an ax raised high above the short man's head.

"Veth," Charles shouted over the roar of the oncoming warrior. "It's just us."

The little furry man skidded to a halt, but he kept his ax raised. "Us who? What's the password?"

Edith frowned. "We didn't make a password, did we?"

Charles shook his head. "No, no we didn't. But we could use an escort, if you don't mind? Edith's hands are a little full."

Veth stepped forward and leaned over as he peered at the little girl beside Edith. He wasn't much taller than she was, but she cowered behind Edith. "What, in the name of all that is evil, is that?"

CHAPTER SEVEN

"My help? Why do you need my help?" Dana's lips puckered as she looked suspiciously at Aidan. "Why do you need to get through the door?"

"I need your help because I've never been through the door. I don't even really know where it is. I just know it's here somewhere. You've been through it. You know how to get to it."

Dana crossed her arms over her chest and raised her chin. "And why would I want to help you? You're clearly in league with the Reformers. Or one of them."

Aidan grinned at her. "You're correct, actually."

Dana glanced over to where her knife lay nearby. Her fingers itched to hold it. It was a frustrating feeling. Her gut told her she could trust him, but her mind kept reminding her that she knew nothing about him. Not to mention the fact that he had very recently held a gun to her head. "You're very proud of that, aren't you?" she spat as she tried to readjust herself casually and put herself in reach of the weapon. She may not need it, but she would still feel more comfortable holding it.

"You're not very good at being sneaky," Aidan said. He reached down and picked up the knife. He examined it a moment, admiring the thin but sturdy construction before flipping it over and hold the handle out to Dana. "Take it if it'll make you feel more comfortable."

Dana eyed him, but reached out to take the knife. She half expected him to shout "Gotcha" and flip it around to stab her, but as her hand closed on the handle, he released the blade and smiled.

"Better?" he asked as she gripped the knife in her hand.

"A little," she said, though she kind of wished she had the gun that he had tucked into the back of his jeans instead of the small knife.

"Good. So now that we've come to the conclusion that I'm not going to try to hurt you—"

Dana raised an eyebrow. "We have?"

Aidan sighed. "I gave you back your knife. Isn't that obvious?"

"No, not really. I've known some Reformers. They can't be trusted. They're sweet to your face, but then they'll turn around and try to ruin your life. Or kill you."

Aidan slapped himself in the forehead. "Right, right. I forgot, I'm sorry." He settled himself back on the floor in front of Dana. "You dated Nethoil, the one who called himself Alex. I had hoped to not have this discussion sitting on the dusty floor of a destroyed diner, but I guess there's no other way around it." He leveled his eyes at Dana. "Everything you know is wrong."

Dana glared at him. *No shit*, she thought, but she wasn't about to tell him that. Ever since the debacle with her ex-boyfriend turning out to be a Reformer and trying to kill them all, she had been able to trust very few people. In fact, the number was so small, she could count it on two fingers: Edith and Edith's mother. She didn't even trust herself completely anymore, especially now that her instinct was telling her to trust this self-proclaimed Reformer. "Is that really how you want to start this conversation?" she asked with a raise of her eyebrows.

Aidan shrugged. "There's no other way to do it. Everything you've been told about Alaesha and the war is wrong." He bobbed his head side to side. "Well, a lot of it, anyway. I'm sure some of it is right."

"You're off to a really good start," Dana said. "Keep going." Her crossed arms and pursed lips said the exact opposite. And yet, despite her sarcasm and biting tone, the

42

more he talked, the more she felt she could trust him. He wasn't a sweet-talker like Alex had been. In fact, he was pretty bad at it. He stumbled over his words and babbled along without actually getting to his point. But that had the strange effect of endearing her to his cause even though she wasn't 100% sure what it was.

Aidan held up his hands. "Okay, okay. Sorry. Let me start again. Yes, I *am* a Reformer. No, I don't want to hurt you, or anyone else. Reformers aren't the bad guys. Not really. I'm sure if you're on the other side, you think we are, but we're not."

Dana rolled her eyes, but a small smile tugged at the corner of her lips. She ducked her head to hide it. "You're not doing any better the second time around," she said. She pulled on her years of experience as a snooty head cheerleader to put a little condescension she didn't actually feel into her words. Aidan was kind of cute in his bumbling way, but she would never in a million years admit that to him or even herself.

"Just hear me out, okay?" He held up his hands in a plea. "It's a lot to explain and I've never had to do it before. Give me a chance to get through it, then you can ask questions and make smart-mouth comments."

Dana's eyes narrowed into a deeper glare, but she pressed her lips into a tight line. She mentally retracted her thought about him being kind of cute.

He gave her a quick nod. "Thank you. So, the war. It's not exactly cut and dry. I'm not sure how much you know, but the Alaeshans, as they call themselves, keep details pretty under wraps. They like to spew their propaganda and not tell the truth."

Dana bristled and a retort burned on her tongue, but she kept her mouth shut. The Alaeshans were people she had known all her life. Her family had been involved with Alaesha in some way for as long as they could trace their lineage back. He wasn't winning her over by making nasty comments that he couldn't back up.

"Reformers aren't just wayward Alaeshans. There are humans in the group, too. A lot of them, actually. I'm part of that group. I'm human. I'm not Alaeshan. I was recruited by a woman named Elva to—"

"Wait, what?" Dana couldn't stop the words from spilling from her mouth. "Elva? Elva Myers?"

Aidan nodded. "Yes, Edith's mother."

"But she's not a Reformer. She helps the Alaeshans."

The man's mouth worked for a moment. "I probably shouldn't have said that. Um, shoot." He ran a hand through his hair. "Like I said, there's a lot more to this than you know."

Dana pointed her knife at him. "You better start talking. Now."

He sighed. "This is not going the way I planned. Okay, what do you know? That might be easier if we start from there. So we're both on the same page, anyway."

Dana continued to glare at him, but she could see the logic in that. So far, all he had done was confuse and frighten her. It wasn't going well for either of them. She was sure she couldn't take him in a fight, and she really didn't want to have to try. Plus, she still trusted him in an odd way.

"I know there's a war between the Alaeshans and the Reformers. The Alaeshans keep the doors guarded and protect the humans, but the Reformers want to open the doors to everyone and enslave the humans."

Aidan shifted when she said that, but he didn't say anything. He just nodded for her to continue.

"The Reformers tried to steal the keys. They did steal the keys, didn't they? They still have one. But the rest are hidden so now no one can get through any door but the Seventh, in Antarctica."

Aidan nodded again.

"Oh, and the doors are smart. They open or refuse to open when they choose. When they think it's important."

Aidan smiled. "Sort of," he said. "What else?"

44

Dana shrugged. "That's about it. When I was in Alaeshan, Reformers attacked the house and tried to kill us so there's no reason for me to trust them. Or you."

"To be fair, your ex wasn't really a Reformer. He was, or called himself one anyway, but he was a rebel even to us. He had his own agenda and was part of a group of people who had evil intentions. Yes, they wanted to enslave humans. They also wanted to bring chaos to Alaesha. Everything they did was to so they could put their wicked leaders in control of both worlds."

"But you don't agree with them?"

"No, I don't. And neither do most Reformers. We call ourselves that because we want to reform things for the better, not for our own gain, but for the good of all. We want to help humans and Alaeshans alike. We want a mutual relationship between the two worlds that isn't controlled by a select few. We want people to be able to move freely and choose their own destiny instead of being forced to live with the one thrust upon them."

Dana frowned. Aidan's words sounded ideal and honest, but could she trust him? She had trusted Alex once and it almost got her killed.

"The Alaeshans, the ones on the other side of the war, they aren't trying to protect the humans, Dana. They're trying to protect themselves. They don't want their old, stodgy way of life to change. They've been in control for so long, they don't want to let go. They want to remain in charge and rule both worlds, the way they have for thousands of years. They only care about themselves."

Dana shook her head. "No. Charles isn't like that. Charles cares about us. All of us. He wants what's best for our world. He wants to take care of us."

Aidan snorted. "He may think he does, but he's as deluded as the rest of them. He grew up in a comfortable, stable way of life, where things were a certain way and never changed. That's how he thinks it should always be, because that's the way it always was. He believes the lies he's been told for centuries. Or he tells the lies himself, I don't know. His world is stagnant, like a pool of water. But you know what happens to stagnant pools of water? They breed blood-sucking mosquitoes."

Dana's frown lost some of its annoyed anger and took on a sad note. "He's a good man," she said, more to convince herself of the truth than him. She didn't know Aidan from a hole in the wall, and Charles had been there her whole life, but deep inside, Aidan's words had a ring of truth. Dana adored Charles, but he was definitely stodgy, an upper class citizen who was confident in his position in the world, both worlds. Did he know the truth? Did he want to know?

"I know this is a lot to take in, but you needed to know the truth."

"I don't know if it is the truth," she said. "My best friend is on the other side of that door, fighting for the Alaeshans. She's killed people to help them, to protect them. Is she fighting on the wrong side?"

Aidan's lips pressed together in a tight line and he shrugged. "Yes, but she doesn't know that. Like you, all she knows is what she's been told, what she's seen. It's not her fault, or yours. You've both been lied to."

"And her mother knew? This whole time she knew what was going on?"

The pain on Aidan's face was almost palpable. "Like I said, it's not my place to talk about that. I can't reveal her secrets. You need to talk to her about that."

Dana groaned and rested her forehead on her knees. "This is so wrong. All of it. I feel like I'm in a book, and I don't even like to read."

Aidan reached over and patted her shoulder. She jerked away instinctively at first, but then let his hand stay there. They sat like that for a few minutes in silence as she tried to digest all the information she had just received.

"So, um, I know I kind of bombarded you with a lot, but I really do need your help."

Dana raised her head. He had a forced smile on his face and was looking at her with the hopeful eyes of a puppy dog wanting a treat.

"What can I do?" she asked.

He stood up and held out his hand. "We need to try to open the door."

"I don't have the key anymore. I can't."

"Like you said, the doors are smart. Sometimes they'll open without the key. You're more likely to be able to get through than I am. And I don't even know where the door is so you'll save me a lot of trouble if you can at least show me."

Dana took his hand and let him pull her to her feet. "If the door doesn't want you to come through, you can't force it. The last time I tried to even touch it without the key, I almost burned my hand off."

"At least show me where it is so I can see it."

Dana sighed. "Okay, this way."

She led him through the maze of rubble and fallen shelves. The wall with the secret tunnel was still intact, amazingly enough, and she found the hidden door with little trouble. Aidan pulled out his cell phone and pulled up a flashlight app. It illuminated the tunnel just enough. Dust and bits of stone littered the walkway, but it was still passable and they found themselves standing at the top of the stairs before long.

"At the bottom," Dana said as she stared into the darkness.

"I'll go first." Aidan pulled his gun out and held it and the cell phone out in front of him. "Stay behind me, just in case."

For the briefest of moments, Dana considered kicking him in the back and running away, but instead she found herself following him down into the darkness. She ran her hand along the wall to keep from stumbling down the steps. When they reached the bottom, tears sprang to her eyes. The door stood there as it had months before, unmarred and safe from the destruction above.

As before, she found her hand drawn to the smooth surface, but unlike before, there was no heat. The last time she had tried to touch the door without the key, a searing pain had waited for her. But this time, all she felt was a coolness emanating from the stone. She laid her hand on the door and it was no different than when she touched the cold stone of a marble counter top.

She realized she had been holding onto a hope that the door would let her through. That hope disintegrated into a million pieces as tears burned her eyes. The door was lifeless and unresponsive. She shoved at it, but it was as if she was pushing on a wall. She ran her fingers down to where the keyhole should have been, but there wasn't one.

"Are you sure this is it?" Doubt was heavy in Aidan's voice.

"Yes," Dana whispered. "This is it." She pressed her cheek against the stone. "It doesn't want us."

"Here, try this." Aidan stepped up beside her and pulled a piece of carved wood from his pocket. "It's how I got through the wards in the diner."

Dana took it. A power emanated from the charm as she placed it against the stone. The hum grew louder for a few seconds. Then sparks burst from the carved symbols.

Dana screeched and dropped the smoking wood to the ground. Aidan picked up the spent charm. "Well, that didn't work."

"Like I said, it doesn't want us." She really had no idea why it would open. Maybe she was trusting the wrong person again, though it had let Alex through when he was with her and Edith. Maybe she was picking the wrong side and the door knew. Or maybe it was too dangerous to go through. Or maybe, just maybe, the door was rejecting her because she had lost the key and let her family and heritage down. Dana placed her hand on the door once more and tried not to cry.

48

CHAPTER EIGHT

Edith scrubbed at her hands. She had been in the bathroom for a good forty-five minutes, but still she couldn't get the feel of death off her hands. They were red and raw, but she kept scrubbing. It didn't matter if she actually touched blood. She could still feel it. She dreamt about it burning the skin from her hands, burying itself deep into her flesh. She continued trying to get the feeling off until a knock sounded on the door.

"Edith?" Mags called from inside the bedroom. "Are you in here?"

The young woman jumped. The knock had barely registered until Mags spoke. Edith turned off the water. "Yeah, in here," she said as she dried her hands.

The bathroom door was open halfway and Mags stepped into the gap. Her eyes narrowed as she looked at Edith. She held out her arms. "Come here, my dear."

Edith hesitated for a moment, but then she practically slammed into Mags. The older woman wrapped her arms around her and held her close. She stroked Edith's hair. "It'll be all right, love."

Edith shook her head. "No it won't. I made such a mistake coming here. I didn't want this. I didn't want any of this." She sobbed into Mags's shoulder. "I'm a killer. A murder. And that's never going to change. I talked to Charles, but it didn't do any good. He's so consumed by all of this. This is his way of life. He just doesn't get it. He doesn't understand." She almost choked on her tears as she pressed her face harder into the older woman's shoulder.

"I know, dear," Mags said as she held Edith close. "It runs in our family unfortunately. Our father was the same way. It left my mother in fits. It does the same to me."

Edith pulled back a bit and looked up at Mags. "You?"

Mags gave her a small smile. "Yes, me. I have my moments too, you know. Not everyone can be strong all the time." She gave Edith a wink and stroked her cheek. "Now let's get you put back together. Charles wants to see you downstairs."

Edith pulled back and groaned. The last thing she wanted to do was see Charles right then. All she wanted to do was crawl in bed and sleep for a week so she could forget about everything.

Mags gave a little shrug. "He does mean well."

Edith sighed. She wanted to believe that, but she wasn't sure anymore. She looked in the mirror. Her eyes were a bit red, but that would fade. She ran her hands through her hair. "Okay, I guess I'm ready."

Mags tucked a loose strand of hair behind her ear and nodded. "Stay strong. Things always work out the way they're supposed to in the end."

Edith smiled and hoped Mags was right. She followed her out into the hall.

Mags gave her another smile and left her in front of her door as she headed in the other direction. Edith looked down the hall toward the stairs. Charles was waiting for her at the bottom. She closed her eyes and took a deep breath. She dreaded what he wanted to talk to her about. The last time she had seen him, he was taking Jilda from her to put the girl who knew where. She hadn't seen the child anywhere and she was afraid to ask. "You can do this," she whispered. "It's fine. It's going to be fine." She plastered a smile on her face and walked down the stairs.

Charles was leaning against the banister at the bottom, chatting with Veth. The furry man looked up as she descended. "Ah, there she is, the lovely Lady Edith."

50

She couldn't help but smile at Veth.

"You wanted to see me?" she said to Charles. She searched his face, looking for some indication of what was to come or what he had done with the girl.

He gave her no clue, nothing to ease her fears. Instead, he held out his hand and helped her down off the last step. "I wanted you to see something you haven't seen yet. Since this is your home now, you should know its ins and outs like I do." He glanced at Veth. "Are you coming with us?"

The other man shook his head. "Not right now. I need to take care of a few things of my own. I'll see you tomorrow at the meeting."

They shook hands and watched as Veth departed. Then Charles held out his elbow. "Shall we?" Edith tucked her arm in his. A knot formed in her stomach as fear and excitement tangled themselves together. He wouldn't tell her where they were going, and she didn't trust his surprises, but she still remembered the time he showed her his secret hiding place in the woods and held on to the hope that this was another surprise like that.

"Right here." Charles stopped in front of a door that Edith had never been through before. He pulled it opened. The stairwell was dimly lit and a musty air wafted up from below. She had been in part of the basement before and it was clean and finished. As she peered down into the darkness, a shiver ran up her spine.

"What is this place?" Her voice echoed down into the black.

"The dungeon." Charles voice held way too much joy.

Edith's eyes went wide and she spun toward him. "You have a *dungeon*? Why?"

"For prisoners," he said, like it was the most natural thing in the world.

"You have a *prison* in your *basement*?"

"Of course. All the Guardians do. And many others of noble blood. It's a common feature in a house such as this."

Edith ran her hand through her hair. "Oh my God," she breathed. Her brain had trouble wrapping itself around this new information.

"What's wrong?" Charles laid his hand on Edith's shoulder. His confusion was evident.

She stared at him. "You have a *prison* in your *basement*," she repeated. How did he not see how ridiculously crazy that was?

Charles shrugged. He clearly didn't get her reaction.

"That's not normal," she said, laying it out for him.

He cleared his throat. "It is. In this world, anyway."

Edith didn't know what else to say. She just shook her head. They were both quiet for a minute as the awkwardness rolled over them.

"Will you come see it?" Charles asked. He stood in the door looking down the stairs.

Edith wanted to say no. She wanted to tell him what a horrible thing it was to have a working dungeon in his basement. But he wouldn't understand. He came from a different world, literally, and things were done differently here. If she wanted to make it in this world, she would need to learn to accept the changes and deal with them. And a strange feeling in her gut told her she needed to see it. She couldn't put her finger on why, but she knew she needed to go down there. She took a deep breath and nodded.

"Okay," she said. "I'll go."

Charles grinned and held out his hand. She took it and as they descended, he gave her a bit more information. "Ours is one of the best dungeons in Alaesha. We have one of the most..." He paused as he searched for the word. "You would call it humane. We treat our prisoners as fairly as can be expected. They all have cots and receive two meals a day."

Edith frowned, but she couldn't argue against it. It was a prison, after all. Cots and two square meals a day was a decent deal. At least it was compared to the vision she had of prisoners rotting in their cells.

The further into the dungeon they descended, the colder it got. "What if they have to go to the bathroom?"

"Each cell has a wooden chamber pot that is emptied every morning."

Edith's nose curled involuntarily. "It doesn't sound very sanitary."

Charles bristled a bit beside her. "It's more than most of the prisoners held here deserve. They're down here for a reason. This isn't a bed and breakfast. They're not on vacation."

Edith's hand slipped from Charles's, but she nodded. She could sort of see his point of view, but she still didn't like it.

The first pair of cells they passed were empty. The doors stood open to reveal the room inside.

"Each cell was carved into the stone and has a magic-enforced door," Charles explained.

Edith poked her head inside. As Charles said, the room contained a cot and a wooden box with a hole in it that served as a toilet. There was nothing else. A small barred window was in each door to allow the guards to look inside, but it was too small for anyone to fit through. Plates of food were slid through a tiny slot at the bottom that was covered with a metal strip when not in use.

They stepped up to the first closed door. The window was so high, Edith had to get up on her tiptoes to see through. A middle-aged woman sat on the cot. Her back was against the cold stone wall and she had her knees against her chest. Her right arm was wrapped up with a bloody bandage.

"How many are here?" Edith asked as they stepped to the next door.

"Five. Plus the scientist."

Edith got up on her tiptoes to look through the window. Her mouth dropped. "Jilda?" Shock froze her where she stood. It was followed by disbelief. The little girl sat in a corner with her arms wrapped around her knees. Her little body shivered as tears fell down her face. She was completely alone. In a dungeon. In Charles's basement.

The disbelief began to fade as anger took over. It raced through her blood and throbbed in her ears. Her fingers itched for her bow. She would nock it with an arrow with Charles's name engraved on it.

She spun on him. Her eyes were wide and she could feel the crazy in them. Her nostrils flared. "You have her in a cell? By herself?"

Charles didn't step back, but he seemed to shrink a bit before her anger. "She's a prisoner, like the rest of them."

His explanation was weak and pathetic. "She's a *child*." Edith practically threw the words at him. She wanted to hit him with them or, even better, her fists.

He said nothing in response. He suddenly found his feet more interesting.

Edith slammed her hand against the wood. "Open this door," she snarled. It took effort to breathe in and out, to keep herself from hitting Charles instead.

Charles looked at her. His mouth opened, but he didn't say anything.

Edith looked down the hall. A guard was sitting on a wooden chair near the middle. "Hey, you," Edith called to him. He glanced up. "Open this door."

The man rose and walked down to them. "Sir?" He looked at Charles.

Charles's mouth was pinched, but he nodded. The man sorted through the key ring on his belt until he found the one he wanted. It slid into the door and the lock clicked loudly. As the door swung open, Jilda's wide eyes found Edith. Her face was streaked with tears and dirt. Edith crossed the space between them quickly. She knelt beside the girl.

"Are you okay?" she asked as she brushed a thumb across Jilda's cheek.

The little girl nodded weakly. "Where's my papa?"

Edith glanced back at Charles. He nodded down the hall. Edith stood up and held out her hand. Jilda hesitated, but she eventually took it. They walked hand in hand out the door.

"Down here," Charles said. He sounded annoyed, but at the moment, Edith really didn't care.

They found the cell the scientist was in. Edith picked Jilda up and let her look through the window.

"Papa!" she cried as soon as she saw her father.

"Jilda!" Gereld jumped off the cot and raced to the door. He put his fingers through the bars to grip those of his daughter. "Jilda, my darling. Are you all right?"

Tears streamed down the little girl's face, but she nodded. "I'm hungry, Papa," she whispered so softly Edith almost didn't hear her.

Edith's heart broke. She glared at Charles. "You said you fed them."

He shrugged. "We do. They get gruel in the morning and bread at night. And water."

Edith closed her eyes. She tried to remind herself that this was a different world with different rules, but it was a tough pill to swallow. In her world, even prisoners had the right to three decent meals a day, proper toilets and sanitary cells. In her world, they didn't lock innocent children up in jail for no reason at all. In her world, none of this would be acceptable.

"I'm taking Jilda upstairs," she declared loud enough for Charles and Gereld to hear.

"No way," Charles said. At the same time, Gereld cried, "Bless you, child."

"Yes, I am," she said to Charles. "You can't keep a child locked down here in these unsanitary conditions. She's done nothing to deserve this."

"She's the child of a Reformer."

"And? How is that her fault? Did she ask to be born into this world? Did she have any choice who her parents are or who you decide to hate? No, she has no control over any of that. All she did was love her family like any child would do. You can't be that cold, Charles. I don't believe that you're that cruel." Edith could feel her anger racing through her veins. How could he not see how utterly unacceptable his behavior was? How could he be okay with all of this? She glared at him with utter disbelief and disappointment. "I can't believe it."

He pressed his lips together in a tight, white line and growled deep in his throat. His eyes narrowed as he looked from Edith to Jilda to Gereld and back again. His nostrils flared. "Fine," he hissed. "But she's your responsibility. You better watch her like a hawk. If anything happens because of her, Boxy will have your head."

"Let her try," Edith snarled. She hated the way Charles could be so easily swayed by the other woman. She had thought Boxy was amazing when she first met the woman, but now she was realizing Boxy basically controlled Charles. Did he have an original thought in his head? Or was he just Boxy's little puppet? "Gereld, I'll take care of her. I promise."

"Thank you," the scientist said as tears rolled down his cheeks. "Thank you. Jilda, darling, be good for the young lady. She's going to keep you safe. Do what she asks. Anything she asks. I'm so sorry I made you a part of this. I'm so sorry."

Edith's heart broke even further. She was watching a father basically say goodbye to his daughter. There was no guarantee he would ever see her again and the regret at ruining her life sat heavy on his face. She set Jilda down and held out her hand. "Come on. Let's go get something to eat."

CHAPTER NINE

"Here you go, my dear." Mags set a tray on the table in front of Jilda and gave the little girl a big smile. "Milk and cookies just for you." She patted her on the head and walked over to sit on the bed beside Edith. "I still can't believe that my brother kept her in the dungeon. I thought something like that would be beneath him." She shook her head. "War changes people."

Edith agreed. "Apparently." She said the word through gritted teeth. She still couldn't wrap her head around the idea that Charles had kept the little girl in the dungeon. Not only in the dungeon, but alone, separated from her father, in a cold, unsanitary cell with nothing but gruel to eat. What kind of man could possibly think that was okay? Edith's stomach sank. And what kind of woman could love that kind of man?

Edith and Mags were silent as Jilda ate her milk and cookies. Her face was still streaked with tears and every so often, she would break down crying, but she seemed a bit more comfortable after an hour in Edith's room, away from the terrors of the dungeon. She had eaten the entire sandwich that Niatha had made for her and devoured a slice of bualdaberry pie.

"I don't know what to do, Mags." Edith didn't look at the woman, but instead stared at the child as she picked a chocolate chip from her glass of milk and popped it into her mouth. She glanced up and caught Edith watching her. Her tiny face broke into a grin and Edith couldn't help but return the smile. It lightened her heart just a bit, a bright spot in a world she no longer recognized.

Mags patted Edith's knee. "All we can do is wait and hope. Hope that this war doesn't last, that it doesn't end us all." She glanced at the timepiece that she always kept tucked in her apron pocket. "I have to go help Niatha with lunch. Do you want anything? I assume you won't be eating with Charles today. He's down in the war room with Boxy again."

Edith rolled her eyes. "What a surprise." The sarcasm dripping from her tongue could have burned holes in the carpet. She was already so irate about the whole situation, she didn't know if she could handle anymore irritation, but hearing that he was once again with Boxy plotting their next move, she found she could manage a bit more anger. She had been so blind to what he was capable of. She didn't know him at all, and she didn't know if she could ever look at Charles the same again. And she definitely didn't want to be anywhere near him right now. "No, I'll eat in here. Maybe just a chicken salad sandwich or something."

Mags bobbed her head. "You got it. I'll be back shortly."

"Thanks."

After Mags left, Edith got up from the bed and walked over to the table. She pulled out the chair opposite Jilda and sat down. "How are the cookies?"

The little girl shrugged. "Okay." She had barely said two words since Edith rescued her from the dungeon.

Edith pressed on. "Niatha is a good cook, isn't he? The pie is delicious."

Jilda nodded and picked at her cookie. She kept her head down and didn't look at Edith.

Edith frowned. Jilda's situation was one she never, ever would want a child to have to go through. The girl's doll lay on the chair between them. Edith picked it up and plucked a piece of dirt from its hair. The doll looked much like Jilda with her striped blue and red hair and eyes the color of sapphires.

58

"My mommy made it for me."

Edith glanced up. The girl was staring at the doll. There had been no word of her mother since the battle. She had not been among the few Reformers that were captured. The rest either fled or lay murdered on the battlefield. Edith didn't want to know where she was, but she had strong doubts that a woman like that would just run away and leave her husband and daughter behind. She would never say that to Jilda, either. The little girl had been through enough. She didn't need that weight on her shoulders, too. Let her hold on to hope that her mother was still out there and would be coming for her and her doll.

Edith set the doll down and put on a brave smile. "Are you finished eating? Would you like to take a bath? Maybe get some of that dirt off you? Mags made you a pretty new dress to wear and some really comfy pajamas. Would you like to try them on?" She stood up and held her hand out.

Jilda hesitated a bit, but eventually she slid off the chair and took Edith's hand. Edith led her to the bathroom. As the warm water filled the tub, Edith collected the clothes and laid them on the shelf in the bathroom. On an afterthought, she went back out into the bedroom and retrieved the doll.

"She needs a bath, too," Edith said when Jilda gave her a questioning look. The doll was indeed covered with the same filth from the dungeon as the girl. At least Charles hadn't been cruel enough to take that away from her.

Edith dumped some foaming wash in the water, and they both watched as colorful bubbles took over the tub. Once it was full, Edith helped her undress and picked her up to put her in the water. She felt extremely uncomfortable until the girl was submerged up to her neck in the bubbles. As she undressed the doll, she couldn't help but laugh at herself. She had basically adopted a child, at least until she could convince Charles to release the girl's father. She would need to get over her awkward feelings if she was going to do right by Jilda.

"Here you go," she said as she handed the doll to Jilda. She grabbed a washcloth out of the closet, along with two big towels and a hand towel. She set the hand towel and one of the big towels aside and laid the other on the floor beside the tub. She knelt down on the towel with the washcloth in her hands.

As she soaked the cloth, Jilda put the doll in the water, but she kept her head out of the bubbles. "Dolly doesn't like her hair wet," she said.

"I see." The corners of Edith's mouth pulled up despite herself. "And what about you? Do you like to get your hair wet?"

Jilda shook her head. "No. The water gets in my eyes. Mama always used a cup. I'd tip my head back and she'd cover my face with one hand so she could wash my hair and it'd stay out of my eyes."

"Your mommy is smart. Wait right here, okay? I'll go get a cup."

The little girl nodded and brushed her doll's hair with a bubble-covered hand.

Edith stood up and left the room, but she kept the door open so she could hear anything out of the ordinary. She grabbed an unused cup from the tray Mags had left on the table and went back into the bathroom. "How's this?"

Jilda shrugged. New tears were rolling down her cheeks.

"Oh, darling," Edith said as she settled back onto the floor. "I know this is hard for you. But I promise I'm going to take good care of you until your daddy can do it again, okay?"

The little girl nodded, but her face was full of disbelief.

"Here, let's get those tears cleaned away." Edith tipped Jilda's chin up with a finger and squeezed the excess water from the washcloth with her free hand. Then she wiped gently at the dirt that stained the child's face. The puffy red eyes remained, but the dirt came away and left her baby skin sparkling and smooth. "That's better." Edith gave her a smile. "Shall we clean the rest of you now?"

Jilda nodded again. As Edith washed the dirt and fear away, she told the little girl about her new home. "You're going to love Ollie. He's a big baby. And he'll love playing with you. I think you're going to be great friends."

She went on to tell Jilda about all the different animals in the barns. The child's face lit up at the mention of the unicorns. "I've never seen a live unicorn before. Mama said they were beautiful. Can we go see them when we get done?"

Edith smiled at her. "Of course. Your mama was right. They're stunning."

The brief light in Jilda's eyes disappeared and her face fell into sadness once again. "We never had unicorns, but we had a gryphon. She was mean. She bit my dog."

"You had a gryphon? I bet that was neat. What was her name?"

"Andola. She died when our house burned."

Edith mentally kicked herself. Of course, Jilda no longer had a home. They were living in a camp in the wilderness in constant fear of being attacked. How could she be so stupid as to bring up such a painful subject?

But the little girl seemed to disagree. "I had the best bedroom in the house," she said. The sadness was still there, but it mingled with a faint smile as Jilda remembered her home. "I could sit in the window and watch the birds flying across the lake. Sometimes, the big ones would swoop down and disappear into the water, then they'd come back up with a fish in their feet."

"That sounds like a nice place to live." Edith picked up a handful of bubbles and placed it on top of Jilda's head.

"It was. Marna lived next door. She was five, but she was still my best friend. We played together all the time."

"Is she still there?"

Jilda shook her head. "Her house burned, too. Her parents went south. Papa said they were going to the Fourth Door. That they were going to the human world. I wanted to go, but he said we were needed in Alaesha still. That we had to stay. We went to the camp."

"How long were you there?" Edith tipped Jilda's head back and covered her eyes with her free hand. Then she scooped up the cup and ran some water over the girl's hair.

"I dunno," Jilda said as she wiped water from her face. "I was three when we got there."

Edith closed her eyes to fight back the sting of tears. She didn't want Jilda to see her cry, but her heart was in pieces for the little girl. "And you're four now?"

Jilda shook her head. Little water droplets flew in every direction. "Four and a half."

"Ooo, you're getting big."

The little girl nodded. "Soon I'll be five." She held up five fingers to prove her point.

"Hmm, do you know when your birthday is? We'll have to celebrate."

Jilda named a date, but the calendar in Alaesha was different than the one in the human world and Edith still didn't have it memorized. She made a mental note to ask Mags later. She finished rinsing out Jilda's hair, and the hair of the doll, and helped them both from the tub. As she wrapped Jilda in the big towel, the little girl looked at Edith with her big, blue eyes.

"What are they going to do to my papa?"

Edith brushed a soggy strand of hair from Jilda's face. "I don't know, sweetheart. I honestly don't know."

The tears started to fall down the child's face once more. "Why? What did papa do? Why are they trying to hurt us?"

Edith pulled her into a hug and held her tight. For a brief second, she considered lying to the child but changed her mind. "They think he's a bad man. They think he's helping some bad people who want to travel to my world and hurt my people."

"The humans?"

"Yes."

Jilda's little head shook fiercely. "He doesn't want to hurt them. He wants to help them."

Edith sat back on her haunches. "Help them?"

Jilda nodded. "He wants to save them. He says the human world is dying and that they need help to save it. He says if the human world perishes, we will, too. But the bad guys, the people in charge of Alaesha, don't want to help. They don't want to open the doors. They want to keep Alaesha separate and keep the humans out. They say they're…" She paused for a moment and her little face pinched as she tried to think of the right word. "I think papa said toxic. The bad people said the humans are toxic and they don't want them here. Papa doesn't agree. Is that why they hurt us?"

Edith didn't answer. Her mind was spinning. "Does your father want to make humans into slaves, to make them work for him for free?"

Jilda brow furrowed as she looked at Edith. "No. Why would he want to do that? Humans are nice, aren't they? Papa always said they were, but I never met one. Until you. And you seem nice. You saved me."

Edith brushed Jilda's hair back and smiled. "I try to be." She grabbed the hand towel and wrapped it around Jilda's head. "Let's get you dried up." She put a smile on her face, but her brain was going in all different directions trying to figure out the new mystery that once again made her question everything she thought she knew about Charles and Alaesha.

CHAPTER TEN

"It's just down here," Dana said as she led Aidan around the corner. She waved her hand in the direction of Edith's old apartment building. "That creepy one on the left. With the broken gate."

He nodded absently as he looked around. Since they left the diner, he never dropped his guard. It made Dana uneasy and she wanted to yell at him and tell him to stop, but she was also partly thankful that he wouldn't relax. She still didn't understand why she trusted him, but she felt safer with him than she had with anyone in a long time.

Aidan moved ahead and stepped into the courtyard. He nodded to Tessa on the stairs as if he'd seen her before. Dana narrowed her eyes at the blind woman. The old lady grinned her toothless grin.

Inside, the apartment building smelled worse than ever. A fresh pile of vomit sat in one corner. "Ugh," Dana groaned. She pressed her sleeve to her nose. "Why doesn't Edith's mom move?"

"It's a good place to hide," Aidan said from up the stairs.

Dana glanced up at him. It was a rhetorical question. She hadn't expected an answer from him, but his comment meant he clearly knew Elva better than she first thought. She needed to find out what was going on.

Aidan knocked on the door in a unique pattern.

"Aidan, I wasn't expecting you," Elva said as she pulled the door open. "I... oh, hello Dana." The woman stopped whatever she was going to say and looked between the two of them.

"She knows, sort of," Aidan explained. "I think it's time we tell her everything."

Elva eyed Dana. The young woman shifted under the gaze. She wasn't sure she wanted to know everything, but if it helped her help Edith, it was totally worth it.

Elva stepped aside and let them both in. She ushered them to the small living room. "Something to drink?"

"Water, please," Aidan said.

Dana shook her head. "No, I'm fine. Thank you." She sat next to Aidan in uncomfortable silence until Elva returned.

A wooden chair was propped next to one wall and Edith's mother grabbed it. She set it in front of the couch so they were in a sort of circle. "Where should we begin?"

Dana shrugged. She looked at Aidan, but he was looking at her. "From the beginning, I guess," she said.

Elva nodded. She had a cup of coffee in her hand and took a sip. She was quiet for a few moments, staring off into space as she gathered her thoughts. "This war has been a long time coming," she began. "It has been brewing since well before I was born. Since before Edith's father was born. There's a huge divide in Alaesha between the old guard, the so-called True Alaeshans and the Reformers who are aptly named."

She paused and took another sip. "Dana, Edith's father wasn't killed by Reformers."

Dana's frown was deep and full of confusion. "He wasn't?"

Elva shook her head. "No. He *was* a Reformer."

Dana gasped. "Oh no. Why would you… what…" A million questions raced through her mind. But the important one popped out. "Does Charles know? Is Edith in danger?"

Elva shook her head again. "No, Charles doesn't know. Edward was undercover. He was a Gathle, one of the oldest families in Alaesha. He had already switched sides when I met him, but he kept his ties with the Reformers a secret so he could work angles only he had access to. He was killed during a secret mission. The Reformers he was with fixed it so he looked like he was murdered by them as he tried to stop them. To preserve his name and protect their work."

"You lied to Edith."

"To protect her. She was in love with Charles. I could see that already, the moment she spoke his name. I couldn't do that to her. I couldn't put her in that kind of risk."

Dana slammed a fist onto her knee. "But she's fighting for the other side. Why would you let that happen?"

Elva narrowed her eyes at the young woman. "Because she is still a human being, and she needs to make her own decisions. If she is meant to, she'll discover the truth. It might be useful having her on the inside."

Dana hissed in contempt. "That's terrible. Using your own daughter like that."

"Dana, we're not using her. She's on her own. Making her own decisions. We have no control over what she does right now. All we can control is what we have in front of us."

"Why are you helping the Reformers anyway? Aren't they trying to enslave us?"

"No," Elva said. She leaned forward and put her free hand on Dana's knee. "They're trying to save us."

"Save us? How? From what?"

"Our world is dying, Dana. Most humans may not see it yet, but it is. And rapidly. We're destroying it. With every new building, every destroyed forest, we're killing our world. The Alaeshans can help us. They can stop that, they can fix what we've done. But the 'True Alaeshans' don't want that. They don't want to help. They want to lock us away and leave us to our fate."

"And the Reformers?"

"They have more advanced magic. They call it magic science. They can save our world. They want to open the doors, even out the populations, allow mingling between the two species, like it's another country instead of another world. They want to teach the humans magic, how to use it to save their own planet, to save themselves."

Dana snorted. "That's ridiculous. Magic can't be taught. It's *magic*. You have to be born with it. You have to already have it. You can't just wake up one day and say, 'Oh, I'm going to do some magic now.' That's not how it works." She waggled a finger at Elva. "You almost had me there. But now I know you're lying."

"I'm not, Dana. Magic isn't mysterious. It is to humans because we don't yet have the science to understand it. The Alaeshans do, though all the scientists are Reformers because the True Alaeshans despise science. They think it's an abomination, a sin. But it's no different than our scientists discovering something new about the world. Some new cure or a way to make our lives better. The Reformers have figured out magic. They can control it, they can teach it. They're even trying to figure out how to open the doors without a key."

Dana's mouth dropped. "Is that possible?"

Elva shrugged. "We don't know, but they're trying. That sort of magic is just a deeper part of the worlds we live in. They've already figured out the smaller magic. It's only a matter of time before they figure out how to open the doors."

"And then what happens?"

"Then people like Charles and Boxy, who want to keep Alaesha separate for themselves, won't have any choice but to open their doors to the humans. They'll have to stop pretending they're trying to protect us, and admit that they're only trying to protect themselves. But they're foolish. If our world dies, theirs won't be far behind. The two worlds are connected. You can't ignore one and hope the other will flourish. That's not how it works."

"So why don't they just come sit in the diner and figure out how to get through the door?"

"First off, all the scientists are in Alaesha so they'd have to get through the door on the other side to get to the door on this side."

"Don't they already have a key? The Seventh Key?"

Elva bobbed her head inconclusively. "Yes and no. They have it and sometimes they're able to use it, but the True Alaeshans are putting up a major fight, so most of the time there's a massive battle going on around the door. There are so few scientists up to the task that it's not worth risking one just to get them through an already opened door."

Dana frowned. This was a lot of information to take in and her head was starting to hurt.

"Plus," Elva continued. "Each door is tuned differently. So getting through one door doesn't guarantee a way to get through the others. They're going to have to work on each door individually. And as you already know, sometimes the doors open of their own accord, so while we may think the scientist has made progress, it's just the door deciding it's time to open and not the actual science that's working."

"This is really confusing," Dana said. She rubbed a hand over her face.

"I know. The world is much more complicated than your history teacher made it out to be."

Dana nodded. "That's for sure. So what do we do now?"

Elva exchanged a look with Aidan. "I think we should try to get through the Third Door."

Aidan shook his head. "Already tried. Didn't work."

Elva's lips pinched and she thought for a moment. "We need to try once more. There's a way through." She glanced at Dana. "I'm sure of it."

Dana's lips curled into a pout. "And what if it doesn't work? What do we do then?"

"I have a plan." Elva rose to her feet. "We're not out of the game yet. Not by a long shot, my dear." She waggled a finger at Dana. "You're a big part of this, bigger than you know. But first, I need more coffee."

She left the room and left Dana wondering what on Earth she could have meant by that.

CHAPTER ELEVEN

Edith held Jilda's hand as they walked through the hall toward the stairs. The little girl was sweaty from playing with Ollie, but the big beast had been as sweet as pie to her. Despite their roughhousing, he had never once hurt her, even accidentally. Jilda had been happy as could be playing with the ginormous puppy and for a few minutes, even Edith had been able to forget her troubles.

"Edith."

She froze. She would recognize that voice anywhere. She held tight to Jilda's hand and turned around. "Charles." Her mouth pressed into a thin line and she couldn't meet his eyes. The anger she had held for him since the trip to the dungeon boiled to the surface again.

A quick glance at his face told her he felt the same. "You need to understand something," he began.

"Oh, don't even." She dropped Jilda's hand and stepped between her and Charles. She pointed her finger toward his chest. Whatever willpower had kept her from exploding before faded and she found herself practically screaming at him. "*You* need to understand something. How could you even possibly think that keeping a *child* in a dungeon was even remotely acceptable? What on earth could possibly possess you to do something so utterly stupid? What kind of person would do something like that?" She ran a hand through her hair and began pacing back and forth.

"I mean, my God. You were treating her like a criminal. What were you thinking? I don't know if I can even look at you anymore. You're so completely..." Her words failed her and she ended her rant with a loud, vibrating growl.

When she finally looked at Charles, his face was red with seething rage. His nostrils flared. "You have no freaking clue, do you?" he said. His voice was rough, like he was doing his best to hold back his anger. "You're such a child."

Edith's jaw dropped and she opened her mouth to defend herself, but he cut her off.

"We're in the middle of a war, Edith. And guess what happens in war? People die. Good people die and good people kill. We do things we wouldn't normally do because that's what we have to do. I thought you got that, but clearly you don't. Maybe you should've stayed in your pathetic little world and let the rest of us take care of it. Boxy--"

Edith scoffed. "Boxy. Always Boxy. Do you even have a thought of your own? Or do you do everything Boxy says?"

"That's not fair."

"No?" Edith spun on him. She finally met his eyes. Hurt lingered behind the anger. "Who's idea was it to keep the little girl in the dungeon? Yours?"

Charles pressed his lips together until they formed a thin white line.

Edith slammed her fists onto her hips. "Well? Was it?"

"No," Charles almost whispered. "It was Boxy's."

Edith snorted. "No surprise there. Did you even try to contradict her? Or did you think it was a good idea, putting a kid in an unsanitary, nasty prison where people have died?" Edith had no idea if people had actually died down there, but she assumed they probably had.

"You are so ridiculous," Charles spat. "I can't even talk to you anymore."

Edith's lips pulled into snarl. "Then maybe it's a good idea you stop trying."

Charles stared at her for a minute before glancing to the little girl cowering behind her. "Better take care of your little pet," he snapped. Then he spun on his heel and stormed off down the hall.

Edith waited until he was gone before she looked at Jilda. Her roaring anger faded almost immediately to be replaced by horrible guilt. The little girl was shaking in fear and tears were pouring down her cheeks. Edith knelt in front of her and pulled her into a hug. "Oh, honey, I'm so sorry. I'm so, so sorry. You shouldn't have seen that." She kissed Jilda's hair and held her until the little girl stopped sobbing. Inside, guilt, anger and fear formed a tight, writhing knot in the pit of her stomach.

CHAPTER TWELVE

Elva pulled a wooden charm similar to the one Aidan used and held it up. A small pop echoed from the back door of the diner. She stepped aside and gave Dana a half-bow as she waved her hand toward the door. "After you, my dear."

Dana's brow puckered, but she already held her little knife in her hand. She opened the door and peered into the murky blackness inside. Nothing had changed.

"Why are we doing this, again?" she asked as she stepped halfway through the door.

"Because we need to get through, and you're a former Keeper, so you're our best shot." Elva held a tiny gun in her hand.

"And what happens if it does work? It's not like we can just waltz into Charles house." Dana stepped inside.

"We'll worry about that when it happens. Where's the door?"

Dana led them through the maze of fallen shelves and destroyed walls. A spider scurried across the floor in front of her as she turned into the tunnel leading to the stairs. "Ick," she muttered. She raised her foot.

Elva grabbed her arm and pulled her back. "Don't. That might be the charm protecting this place."

"A spider?"

The older woman knelt down and picked up the bug as it began to climb the wall. It squirmed in her hand. She held it by one leg and dangled it in front of Dana's face. "Look closer."

Shivers rolled up Dana's spine. She glanced at the spider. And realized it wasn't a spider. It was a tiny round black marble with six spindly string legs. She peered closer at the creature. It had no spidery features aside from the legs and body. "How is it even moving?"

Elva smiled. "Magic."

"And that protects this place?"

"There are probably several of them. Spread out throughout the diner. They likely each have their own territory that they patrol. It's a good bet that whoever put them there knows we're here."

Dana couldn't help but glance around, even though they were in the dark tunnel and couldn't see more than a couple feet in front or back of them. "Is that a good or bad thing?"

Elva shrugged. "That depends entirely on who these belong to." She glanced back at Aidan, who was watching the path behind them. "But it's probably a good idea to get moving. We don't want to be caught dawdling by the wrong person."

Dana gripped her knife tighter and moved toward the stairs. As she descended into the depths beneath the diner, she saw more spiders skittering across the ceiling. How did she miss them before? She had no idea. Maybe they didn't want to be seen. Or maybe she was too concerned about Aidan.

She reached the door and stopped in front of it. Unlike before, it was no longer cool. A warmth emanated from it and called to her. Dana raised her hand.

"Wait," Elva said as she grabbed Dana's arm. "Don't burn yourself."

Dana glanced at her, but pulled her hand back. Elva waved her hand in front of the door. "This isn't good. You said the last time it was cold. Why is it so hot now?"

"It's working," Dana said. She couldn't hide the smile from her face. The door was finally responding. It was beckoning her like an old friend. Her heart pounded and her skin felt warm as joy raced through her. She raised her hand again. Her fingers tingled and ached. She moved her hand toward the door, fearing the burning pain that it threatened, but the warmth never changed. It was like a spring sun on a cool day. Her fingers touched the stone. Elva gasped, but Dana didn't remove her hand. She pressed her palm to the door. A light pain ignited her nerves, but she kept her hand where it was. A minute passed.

"Dana, are you okay?" Elva put her hand on Dana's shoulder.

The younger woman nodded. "It's accepting me."

"How do you know that?"

Dana shrugged. "I feel it."

Elva shared a worried glance with Aidan, but neither of them said anything. Two minutes later, a faint crack echoed through the door. And then it started to move. It slid open to reveal the tunnel behind. Dana stepped back. Her mouth stood open in a perfect circle. She stared into the blackness.

"You did it," Elva whispered. She turned to Aidan. "She did it."

They both cheered and clapped Dana on the back. For her own part, her excitement was tainted with a fear and worry that had been with her since Edith left. Would she see Edith again? How would her friend react when she walked through the door on the other side? Would Charles know something was wrong? What would he do? How could she tell Edith what was really going on?

Dana stepped through the door. The first torch lit up of its own accord. She walked down the long tunnel in a daze, her feet following a path she knew by heart. They walked for a long time. It seemed much longer than any of the other times she had been to Charles home, but it was a special occasion. Her stomach roiled and her head swam. A million questions raced through her mind, none of them with an obvious answer. She gripped her knife so tight, her hands began to ache.

Elva and Aidan were quiet behind her. They sensed her fear, her excitement. They followed with their weapons drawn, both unsure of what they would encounter at the end.

Would they be welcome? Would Charles know the truth? Would they be slaughtered on sight? None of them knew what would happen. All they knew is that the door finally opened. It finally let them through.

As they rounded the last corner, Dana froze. Elva bumped into her. "Dana? What's wrong?"

Dana raised her knife. "The key. It's in the door."

Sure enough, the key Edith had owned sat there, sticking out of the lock, beckoning to them.

Elva moved forward and peered at the key. "Why is it in the door on this side?"

Dana shrugged. "I have no idea." Her mind raced. Why was Edith's key in the door? Why was it just sitting there, untouched? Was Edith okay? Did something happen to her? Did the key refuse to let her touch it since it was supposed to belong to someone under eighteen? Did she just abandoned it? Not a single logical explanation presented itself. She couldn't imagine why Edith would just leave the key there.

"You're sure that's the key?"

Dana nodded. "I'd know that key anywhere." She had held it in her possession for a decade. Even just looking at it now, she could feel it in her hand. She could imagine the cool metal on her skin, the tiny vibration as it clicked in the lock.

"Should we open it?" Aidan moved his hand toward the key.

Elva grabbed his wrist and pulled him back. "Don't. Let Dana do it. You have no relationship with it. It might hurt you."

Aidan frowned, but he moved back behind the women.

Dana stepped forward. Her heart pounded so heart in her chest that it began to hurt. She had no idea what would happen. She was eighteen. The key was supposed to belong to someone seventeen or under. And it had abandoned her before. Would she be hurt if she tried to use it? Would it do anything at all? Was it really just a plain key and her child's imagination was getting the better of her?

75

She closed her eyes and took a deep breath. Shivers raced up her arm as her hand closed around the key. She almost jerked back out of pure instinct, but she made her fist close all the way. Nothing happened. No sparks of electricity jolted her body. She didn't suddenly fall down dead. It was just a normal key. A thread of disappointment wriggled through her mind. The key she had been trained to respect, to revere, wasn't anything special. It was just a plain, old key. She turned it. A faint click echoed in the tunnel. Her eyes brightened and she looked back at Elva. Smiles blossomed on all their faces.

"You did it," Elva cried. "Open it. Go ahead." She stepped forward just behind Dana. Her gun was still raised, but there was an unrivaled excitement in her eyes.

Dana turned back to the door and took a deep breath. What would she find on the other side of the door? Would Charles and Edith welcome them? Would they even be there? She put one hand on the knob and turned. It spun in her hand like it should have. She put her other hand on the door and with the blood racing through her body, she pushed.

Nothing happened.

Nothing at all.

The door didn't budge. She tried again. It still wouldn't move. She turned the key and turned it again. The lock still clicked. The handle still turned. But the door would not open.

"What's wrong?" Elva was right beside her now. The excitement had turned to concern. "Why isn't it opening?"

Dana shook her head. Tears stung her eyes. "I don't know. It just won't move." She put her shoulder to the wood and pushed. It was as useful as trying to push a skyscraper. The door simply wouldn't move. Fat drops of salty water rolled down her cheeks. "It won't open," she cried. She pulled the key from the lock and held it in her hands. "Why? Why won't it open?"

Elva squeezed her shoulder gently. "I don't know." She rested her head on Dana's. "I just don't know."

Dana tried one more time. It didn't work. Elva patted her on the back. "Come on," she said. "Let's go back."

Aidan leaned in. "What if it doesn't let us out the other way?"

Dana's eyes went wide. Elva's lips tightened. "We'll worry about that if it happens. Let's go." She pushed past him and led the way.

Dana watched them disappear around the corner. She looked back at the door. Edith was on the other side of that door, fighting a war for the wrong people. She could be killed for the wrong reasons, thinking Charles was a good guy, thinking she was giving her life for a good cause. Dana's nostrils flared. "Edith could die," she whispered. How did that never occur to her before? Why did she let Edith go into Alaesha in the middle of a war? What was she thinking? Before she knew what she was doing, her fist slammed into the wood. "Edith!" she shouted as loud as her voice would carry. "Edith, open up! Edith." She beat at the door with both hands and screamed at the top of her lungs.

"Dana!" Elva's hands wrapped around Dana's shoulders and pulled her backward. "Stop. Don't do that. You'll hurt yourself." She hugged Dana tight and stroked the sobbing girl's hair. "It's okay. We'll find a way through. We'll see her again."

"How do you know that?" Dana cried. "How do you know?"

"I don't. But I have hope. And that's all we can have right now. The door won't let us through, so I doubt it would let her through, either. We need to go."

Dana sniffed and glared at the closed door. She grabbed the key and stuffed it in her pocket before trudging after Elva down the long, dark tunnel.

CHAPTER THIRTEEN

"Do you have a four?" Edith eyed the little girl sitting cross-legged across from her on the bed.

Jilda's face puckered in concentration as she peered at her hand, carefully hiding it from Edith's view. After a few seconds, a big smile crawled across her face and she loudly declared, "Nope. Go Fish!"

Edith gave her a fake glare and plucked a card from the pile. It was a match to one of her other cards, but she stuck it in her hand and growled. "Aw, man. Nothing. Your turn."

Jilda giggled. "Do you have a six?"

The card Edith had just pulled was indeed a six. She removed it from her hand and handed it to Jilda. The little girl matched it with one of the two cards she held and put it on her ever-growing pile. "Only one more," she bragged as she waved the card in front of Edith's face.

"You are much too good at this game. I should have never taught you how to play. Now I'll never win again." Edith put on a pretend pout that just made Jilda giggle even harder. She examined her hand again. "Do you have a two?"

Jilda's arm shot out as she practically threw the card at Edith. "Here you go." She looked at her pile of pairs. It was more than double the size of Edith's. "I win," she cried as she jumped up and bounced on the bed. Her hands clapped together and the smile on her face made Edith's heart melt.

"Yes, you certainly did." Edith put all the cards in a pile and climbed off the bed. She looked out the window. It was a bright, clear day. Ollie was playing in the back yard. "Do you want to go out and see Ollie?"

They had seen the big puppy earlier that morning, but they hadn't had time to do more than pet him before breakfast.

The little girl's hands clapped together. "Oh, yes. Can I ride him?"

Edith laughed. "He's not a horse. He's a dog."

Jilda shrugged. "He's a big dog."

Edith nodded in agreement. "That he is. We'll have to ask him if he'd mind. Let's get your shoes on." Edith grabbed the tiny red sandals that Mags had found for Jilda. Jilda swung her feet over the bed and dangled her toes in front of Edith. She giggled when Edith tickled her feet.

Once the shoes were on, Edith stood up and held out her hand. "Ready?"

Jilda bounced to the floor and slipped her fingers through Edith's. "Uh huh."

They spent the rest of the day outside, chasing Ollie, playing in the stream and visiting the unicorns. Ollie was even kind enough to let Jilda climb on top of him as he was laying down chewing on a bone. Edith grinned and wished she had a camera to capture all of the fun moments the little girl was having. She was also a bit envious the little girl seemed to so easily forget all the horrible things that had happened to her and could enjoy the little things in life so much.

For the past week, she had been avoiding Charles as much as possible. She still cared about him. At least, she cared about the man she had thought he was before. She just couldn't wrap her head around the fact that he was capable of doing some horrid things that she simply could not accept. Their explosive argument in the hallway niggled at the back of her mind. She had seen him once since then. Their eyes met across the hall for the briefest of seconds before he turned around and went back the way he had come. He was avoiding her as much as she was avoiding him, and she felt a bit of relief at that. They needed to talk and figure out their problems, but she couldn't, not yet. She wasn't ready.

That night, as she tucked Jilda into bed, Edith couldn't help but feel a bit lighter. The little girl had given her a purpose, a hope. She read Jilda a story and pulled the covers up around her neck.

A knock sounded on the door. Edith and Jilda both glanced up. Edith gave her a little kiss on the forehead before going to answer the door. "Get to sleep," she jokingly admonished the child.

Charles was on the other side of the door. Tension knotted Edith's shoulders and her chest tightened. She didn't want another fight. She couldn't handle it right then.

He looked into the darkened room. "She's asleep?"

Edith nodded with her teeth clenched together. "She will be soon."

He tipped his head down the hall. "Can we talk? Please?"

Edith glanced back at Jilda, but the little girl had worn herself out and she was already deep in dreamland. She pulled the door shut behind her. She followed Charles to the stairs where he settled onto the top step. She hesitated a moment before sitting down beside him. His posture wasn't angry. It was more sad than anything. A bit of Edith's own anger melted away. "What's wrong?" she asked.

Charles poked at a hole in the carpet, a burnt reminder of the chaos that had found the house only recently. "You're getting pretty close to the girl, aren't you?"

Edith gave him a sidelong look. She shrugged. "I guess. Why?" She wasn't about to tell him that the only thing keeping her sane at the moment was her interaction with Jilda. The girl gave her a purpose, a good purpose. She needed that right now.

He pulled a string from the carpet and examined it. "I'm not sure that's such a good idea."

She turned to face him and narrowed her eyes. "Why?"

He snorted. "I feel like I'm talking to a two-year-old."

Edith glared at him with her mouth open. "Wow, you're kind of a jerk." The anger that was receding came back in full force.

"No, no." Charles held up his hands. "I didn't mean it like that. It was the 'why, why' thing. You know? When a kid doesn't understand something, they just keep asking why, why the whole time until you get so frustrated, you give up."

Edith's eyes narrowed further, but she kept her anger in check. "And what's your point?"

Charles sighed. "I didn't... I'm just worried, that's all. She's the daughter of a scientist."

Edith crossed her arms and shook her head. "She's a four-year-old child who had no say in being a part of this stupid war. She's too young to know much about what's going on, and it's not fair that she was dragged into it like this."

"She's a Reformer, Edith. Born and raised. Just like the rest of them. Just because she may seem cute now, it doesn't mean she won't grow up to be a rebellious murdering psychopath like all the others."

"Rebellious murderous psychopaths? Is that what they all are?" An ironic smile pulled at Edith's lips.

Charles stared at her. "Yes. You've seen them. You've seen what they can do." He waved a hand in the air. "Look at what they did to my house. You were here when it happened."

"I have seen some of them. A small contingent. But Jilda's father seems nice enough."

"He tried to *kill* me, Edith."

She shrugged. "After you tried to kill him first."

"What has gotten into you? Are you really that naive that spending time with a Reformer child can completely brainwash you?"

Her mouth dropped open and she stared at him. Her eyes began to sting. "Did you really just say that to me?"

He stood up. "Yeah, I did. You're letting your judgment be clouded by a kid. You're ignoring the whole reason you came to Alaesha in the first place."

She stood up, too. Their voices were rising as they spoke. "I came to Alaesha to be with *you*. I came to this world for *you*. Nothing else. I gave up everything for you, and I barely even see you anymore. All you care about is this stupid war and making sure you win."

"This stupid war? This stupid war will decide the fate of both of our worlds. If we don't win, your people become slaves. Is that what you want?"

"I'm not sure I believe that anymore. Jilda says her father is trying to help humans. He's trying to use magic science to make both of our worlds better places so we can all live together in peace."

Charles laughed and ran a hand through his hair. "I don't believe this. Are you seriously taking the word of a four-year-old Reformer over me? You can't be that stupid."

The tears flooding into Edith's eyes burst over her lashes. "You are so mean," she whispered. "I want to go home."

Charles scoffed. "Well, maybe you should've figured that out before you left the key on the other side of the door."

They glared at each other for a minute. Edith's head swam and her heart hurt. She wanted to take Jilda and go back to her world, where she at least knew some of what was going on.

Charles rolled his eyes and snorted. "I have things to do. Go play with your new doll." He turned away and stomped down the steps.

Edith watched him disappear before she sank down on the stairs. She cupped her face in her hands and let the tears flow freely. She cried until she couldn't cry any more, then she walked down the hall and opened her door as quietly as she could.

Jilda was already asleep. She had one arm wrapped around her doll. The other gripped the edge of her pillow.

Edith crawled in beside her. Jilda whimpered and shifted into her arms. Edith held on to her the rest of the night, focusing on the only thing she was certain of anymore.

CHAPTER FOURTEEN

Dana held the key in her hands and ran her fingers over the smooth metal. She had held the key many, many times before, but this was the first time she really, truly felt it. It had always been a part of her life, part of her being. From the time she inherited it from her cousin at age five, the key had been with her. She had never let it go, never parted from it. Until the day it disappeared. That day had changed everything, her whole life, everything she knew.

And now the key was in her possession once again. Only this time, it wasn't hers. Who did it belong to? She had no idea. Edith was officially eighteen. The key was no longer hers. It had been left abandoned in the lock in a buried tunnel between two worlds. Did the rules still apply? If they did, Dana shouldn't be able to hold the key as she was. It should be burning her, or at the very least, trying to escape. And yet, it lay in her hands as inert as a plain old everyday object.

"Here, drink this." Elva sat down beside Dana on the couch and handed her a mug.

"What is it?"

"Tea. Tea makes everything better."

Dana raised an eyebrow, but she took a sip. It was delicious. Sweet, but not too sweet, with subtle notes of cranberry and apple. It tasted like autumn in a cup.

Elva smiled. "See?"

Dana laughed. "Well, things are still poop, but the tea is good."

"And you laughed." Aidan sat on the other side of her and poked her softly in the ribs with his elbow.

"Yeah, well..." Dana's face fell into a frown again as she looked at the key in her other hand. "We still don't know how to get through the doors. How to find Edith. Why did it let us through the first one but not the second? Why would it do that?"

Elva shook her head. "I don't know, Dana. I'm only human and the magic doesn't make all that much sense to me. Sometimes, it does things that we can't understand."

Dana sighed. "That's so annoying."

Aidan laughed. "Yeah, it is. Can I see it?"

Dana's forehead puckered and for a moment, the old protectiveness came back to her. Her fingers tightened around the key and she almost put it back into her pocket. Then her shoulders sagged and she held it out. As Aidan reached for it, a small hope sparked in the back of Dana's mind that the key would rebel, that it would shock Aidan or burn him, that it would choose to stay with Dana instead of going to someone else.

That hope fizzled and died as his fingers plucked it from her palm. He examined it thoroughly. What he was looking for, Dana didn't know, but he clearly didn't find what he wanted.

"Hmmph. Whatever magic it had before is gone, it seems. It's just a lump of metal now. Just a boring old key without a lock." Dana was mildly surprised when he handed it back to her.

She grabbed it and stuffed it in her pocket. It might just be a key, but she still wanted it. She still needed to protect it in any way she could.

"So what's the plan now?" Aidan sipped his own cup and looked at Elva over the brim.

"We go to Chile."

Dana choked on her tea. "What?"

"We go to Chile. Santiago to be more specific."

"You mean, like, another country?"

Elva raised her eyebrows and smiled. "Yes, Chile is another country. On another continent, even."

Dana's mouth worked like a fish, but nothing came out. "What's wrong?"

"I, uh." She rubbed a hand across the back of her neck. "I've never been out of the US."

Aidan and Elva exchanged a glance. "Seriously?" Aidan asked. "Your parents have a ton of money. I would've though you'd traveled all over."

Dana shook her head. "No. We didn't leave America. Since I had the key, we never went too far away from the door."

"Have you ever been on a plane?" Aidan looked at her with a strange sort of skepticism.

Dana shrugged. "Once? Maybe twice?"

"Do you have a passport?" Elva asked.

Dana shook her head. "No. I've never needed one. You don't need a passport to get into Alaesha."

"Yet," Aidan said.

"Yet," Elva repeated with a smile.

"So what do I do?" Dana asked.

Elva patted her knee. "Don't worry. I can take care of that. I'll get you a passport that'll pass all inspections."

"Okay." She looked into the swirling depths of her tea. "Um, why are we going to Chile, anyway?"

"That's where the Fourth Door is. The Reformers control it on the Alaeshan side. And there's a big contingent of humans helping them on this side. It's the next best place to try to get through now that we know we can't get through here."

Dana's face puckered. "I have a question."

"Okay, go ahead." Elva looked at her expectantly.

"What would we have done if we did get through on this side?"

Another glance was exchanged between Elva and Aidan. Aidan answered. "We would have used the opportunity to take the Third Door."

"Charles would never have allowed that," Dana said.

"He wouldn't have a choice if we had enough manpower."

Dana bit her lip. "And what about Charles?"

Aidan shrugged. "Depends on how hard he tried to fight us."

Dana's heart sank, but she was secretly grateful the door didn't open. If it had, she could be in the middle of battle right now. Or worse, standing over the corpse of a man she had known and trusted her whole life, or his sister's, or even her best friend's. She shuddered and thanked whoever was listening for not answering her earlier prayers. She didn't like how they talked about Charles like he was just another Alaeshan on the wrong side of the war, but she knew he had little sympathy for the Reformers. He would have said the same, had the roles been reversed. And the truth was, she found herself trusting Elva and Aidan more than she had ever trusted Charles, and she had known the man her whole life. Her gut was telling her this was the right path.

"So now what?" she asked.

"Go home and get packed. Not too much, please. A small suitcase at most. We're not going to check any bags if we can help it."

"Okay. What do I need?"

Elva shrugged. "Clothes. Comfortable ones. That's about it." She glanced down at Dana's strappy sandals. "And sneakers if you have them."

Dana frowned. "I might? I think I have one pair that isn't covered in grease. I'll see if I can find them." She stood up and handed the cup back to Elva.

"Meet us back here in a few hours. I should have everything ready by then."

"Really? That quick?"

Elva smiled. "I know some people who work fast." She gave Dana a wink.

The younger woman tried to mimic the smile, but it came out as more of a grimace. Since she'd met Aidan, her world had pretty much turned upside down, yet again. Her stomach was trying to copy it. "Okay, I'll meet you back here."

Elva gave her a quick hug before Dana scampered out the door. An hour and a half later, she was standing in her living room next to a small pink travel bag, arguing with her parents about her impending trip.

"You don't even know these people, Dana. What are you thinking?"

"I have to do this, Dad. It's the right thing."

"It's not. You know what Charles said about Reformers. They can't be trusted. None of them can."

"And how do you know you can trust Charles?"

"Because he's known our family for generations."

"That doesn't mean anything. Has he ever let us into his world? Have we ever seen any of it? Talked to anyone else?"

Her father growled. "Dana, don't be stupid. You have no money, no passport. What if you get stuck down there? What are you going to do then? You're not going and that's final."

Dana's nostrils flared. "I'm eighteen, Dad. There's nothing you can do about it."

"As long as you're under my roof—"

"Ned, please shut up." Dana's mother sighed and cupped her daughter's cheeks. "Are you sure about this, dear?"

Dana nodded. "Yes, Mom. I am. I feel it. It's what I need to do."

Her mother's lips puckered as she stared into her eyes. They stood like that for what felt like an eternity. "Okay. Then I trust you to do the right thing. Ned, give her some money."

"What? No. I won't support this. I'm not—"

Her mother sighed again. "Ned..."

A glare and a grumble later, her father was pulling his wallet from his pocket. He pulled out a wad of cash. "This is all I have out of the bank."

Dana counted it. It was $673. She looked at her mother. "Are you sure? This is a lot of money."

Her mother folded the bills into Dana's hands and gripped them tightly. "If it's used for good, it's worth it."

"This—"

Her mother held up her hand and stopped whatever protest her father was going to make. "Be careful, Dana. And please let us know when you get there." She kissed her daughter on the cheek. "I love you."

Dana smiled and her eyes began to tear up. "Thanks, Mom. I love you, too." She gave her a hug and turned to her father. "Dad…"

The man glared at her for a moment, but then his arms opened wide. "Come here," he growled. As he wrapped her into his arms, he said, "Be safe. I won't have my only daughter come home hurt."

"I will."

He kissed her on the forehead. "If you need anything at all, call us. We'll be here."

She nodded. With one final look, she closed the door behind her and wheeled her suitcase down the sidewalk. She walked a quarter of the way to Elva's apartment before plopping on a bench. She didn't want to spend any money unless she had to, but her feet hurt. She had managed to find a pair of barely worn sneakers that weren't marred by the dirty fry grease from her horrid job, but she had packed them into her suitcase and put on the sandals she had worn before. The lack of support was taking a toll on her feet and her heels were beginning to ache.

A few minutes later, a bus stopped. She climbed aboard with her suitcase and dropped the required toll into the little black box by the door. The driver dropped her at the end of the street and she rolled her suitcase the rest of the way to the apartment building. Tessa was on the steps as she walked up.

"Hey, Tessa," Dana greeted her as she began to move around the old woman.

Before she could get by, Tessa's fingers snaked out and gripped her wrist. Dana gasped and looked down. The woman's other hand was out and flat. In her palm lay a small elaborately braided key chain with a pretty little charm on the end.

"Is that for me?" Dana asked.

Tessa nodded.

Dana smiled, though she didn't think the lady could see it. "Thank you, Tessa. That's so sweet." She took the key chain and attached it to the key in her pocket. "It's beautiful."

Tessa grinned and released Dana's arm. Dana went inside.

Elva and Aidan were waiting for her when she got to the apartment. Two bags stood by the door and a pile of papers lay on the kitchen counter.

"All ready?" Elva asked as Dana entered.

"Yeah, I think so."

"Good. Let's go." Elva grabbed the papers.

"Wait, my passport?" Dana raised her eyes hopefully.

Elva pulled a blue booklet from the pile and handed it to her. Dana opened it and peered inside. Her class photo stared back at her. "Dana Myers?"

"It's much easier that way. Then I can just fill out your forms for you and you won't have to worry about anything."

"What about my driver's license? It doesn't match."

Elva pulled another item from the pile and handed it over. "Good catch. Leave yours here. You can get it when we come back."

Dana pulled her license out of her purse and replaced it with the new one. "Is Aidan my brother?" she joked.

"Boyfriend," Aidan said with a grin.

Dana's mouth dropped. "Seriously?" The last boyfriend she had had tried to kill her. She didn't want to date Aidan, or even pretend to date him. "No, uh uh. No way."

"It's the easiest and most plausible explanation," Elva said.

Dana's nose curled. "I don't want a boyfriend."

"Oh, come on," Aidan said. He threw an arm around her shoulder. "I'm not so bad." He gave her a wink.

She groaned and looked at Elva. "Do I have to?"

Edith's mother laid her hand on Dana's shoulder. "It's just pretend. And you only have to worry about it if someone asks. It's not a big deal."

Dana frowned, but she nodded her ascent. They all picked up their bags and Dana followed Elva out the door.

A cab was waiting for them when they got downstairs. Elva and Aidan seemed to be pros at moving through the airport and in no time at all, Dana found herself seated by the window in a row of three seats. Aidan sat next to her and Elva was on the outside of the row.

As the plane rolled down the runway, Dana's fingers turned white around the armrests. Aidan patted her knee. "You'll be fine. More people die riding bikes each year than airplanes."

"That doesn't mean it won't be us," Dana grumbled.

"Here," he said. "Look at this. It might help distract you." He pulled the catalog out of the back of the seat in front of them.

It did help a bit and before Dana knew it, they were into the air and soaring along nicely. "Ooo, that's neat. I want one of those." Dana pointed to an inflatable pillow in the catalog.

With a grin, Aidan reached into the small knapsack he had stuffed under the seat in front of him and pulled out a crumpled piece of velvety plastic. He blew into the air hole and popped the pillow behind Dana's head. "Ask and you shall receive, my dear."

Pink crept into her cheeks as a smile tugged at her lips. "Have any other cool toys in there?"

"Not really. Just a tablet, change of clothes, stuff like that."

"A tablet? I didn't think you could bring that stuff on a plane."

Aidan laughed. "This isn't the 50's." He pulled it out. "Want to watch a movie?"

"Sure."

He pulled out two sets of headphones and plugged them into the dual audio ports on the tablet. Then he let Dana select a movie. They spent the rest of the flight with their heads pressed together, alternately watching and picking on each other.

Elva sat beside them, fighting the knowing grin that kept creeping across her face.

CHAPTER FIFTEEN

"That's it?" Dana stared at the door in front of her.

"Yep. That's it," Aidan said from beside her.

Elva was already in the cafe across the street, finding a table for them all.

"But it's so... plain." Dana glanced around. "And obvious."

"What's obvious about it?"

"It's in the middle of the street. And it's bright red."

Aidan snorted. "It's not in the middle of the street. It's in a house that happens to be next to two other houses. And if you'll notice, all the houses on this street are brightly colored." He pointed to the house next door. "That one is blue. The one on the other side is yellow. The one over there is green."

"Yeah, but..." The words disintegrated in her mouth as she stared at the Fourth Door. "It should be hidden."

Aidan shrugged. "Why?"

Dana lowered her voice to a hiss. "Because it leads to another world, duh."

His grin returned. "And how would anyone know that from just looking at it. Do you see anything that screams 'Hey, walk through me to get to another dimension?' No. There's nothing that makes it stand out like that."

"But what if someone who doesn't know any better goes up and touches it? What about salesmen and Girl Scouts and all the random people who come to your door to try to get you to give them money? They'd get burned and then there would be all sorts of trouble."

"The Guardian thought of that a long time ago. See that door hanger?" He pointed to the wooden knocker in the shape of a screaming monkey. Dana nodded. "It's a charm. It does a lot of what the ones at the diner do. People look right over it. Most don't even register that there's a door there. They think it's just part of one of the other houses. They just pass right by."

"Yeah, but what if someone does touch it?"

"The door doesn't respond. It acts just like a regular door."

"How is that possible?"

"Watch." He walked up the steps and reached toward the bright red door.

"Aidan, no!" Dana clapped her hands over her mouth and bit back on a scream as his hand touched the wood.

"Ahhh!" he cried.

The scream burst from her lips. People walking past her on the street stopped and stared. Aidan began to laugh.

"I'm just kidding," he said as he bounced down the steps. "I'm fine. Look." He held out his hands for examination. He was indeed just fine, though Dana's heart was thumping in her chest and her cheeks burned from the attention brought by her unexpected screech.

"You're such a jerk." Dana punched him in the arm as hard as he could.

"Ow," he cried. "You punch like a girl."

"Good." She crossed her arms and glared at him.

He rubbed his arm, but his smile returned. "Come on. Let's go find Elva." He led the way across the busy street to the cafe. "This is where they all hang out."

"They?"

"The people that watch the door."

Dana's face crunched up. "I'm so confused."

He held the door open for her. "What's confusing?"

"I dunno. I guess I expected a camp and a big wall or army or something. I mean, there's a war going on.

94

Shouldn't people be fighting and stuff? How are they protecting the door?"

Elva waved to them and they walked over to the table she had found in a corner. Two other people were sitting with her. As Dana and Aidan joined them, Elva made introductions. "Dana, Aidan, this is Gisella and Nikolaus. They're in charge of the door."

Dana sat down. "Just the two of you?"

Nikolaus laughed. "No. There are many of us, but we don't make it obvious. We're not going to line up in a barricade in front of the door like a bunch of fools. What? Did you think we would?" He grinned good-naturedly at her.

She shrugged. "Well, kinda…"

Gisella glared at Nikolaus. "Don't pick on her. Things are different up there." She turned to Dana. "There are many of us, but we remain undercover. Do you see the man outside selling flowers?"

Dana looked out the window. Up the street, half a block down from the Fourth Door, a man stood next to a wooden cart loaded with flowers. "Yeah."

"He's one of us. So are all the baristas here, the owner of this cafe, nearly everyone who works in that restaurant next door, and the people who own the houses on either side of the Door. Plus, this area is frequented by Reform supporters. The Door is well protected, though it may not be obvious to one who does not know about us."

Dana frowned, but she nodded.

"It works in our favor," Elva explained. "The Alaeshans are loathe to draw attention to themselves, so they're less likely to attack out in the open. And since this area is well populated and the door is in a very obvious place, it's more protected than, say, the Third Door, which is hidden inside a diner under the floor."

"Yeah, I guess that's true," Dana conceded. "If they tried to start a war in the streets here, it'd be a whole big mess."

"Exactly."

"Can I get you anything to drink?" A young woman walked up to the table as they were talking.

"Valentina," Gisella greeted her. "This is Dana and her boyfriend Aidan."

Dana opened her mouth to protest, but Elva reached over and squeezed her knee. She gave her a little shake of the head.

Valentina smiled at them. "What would you like to drink?"

Dana glanced at Elva. "I don't really drink coffee."

"Bring her a Cafe Bombon," Gisella suggested.

"What's that?" Dana's nose curled in concern.

"It's half espresso, half sweetened condensed milk. You'll like it."

"Okay, that sounds good." She looked up at Valentina. "I'll take that."

The barista nodded. "And for you?" Her smiled brightened a bit as she looked at Aidan.

"I'll have the same," he said. "Thanks."

Valentina gave him a brighter smile and walked away. Dana raised her eyebrows at Aidan. He just grinned at her.

"Elva says you have a key?" Nikolaus asked when Valentina left.

"Yeah." Dana reached into her pocket and pulled it out. "It was just sitting in the door."

He and Gisella looked it over quickly before handing it back to Dana. "Put it away. Keep it hidden."

Dana looked at Elva. "I thought we were safe here."

"We are, but there are still spies everywhere. It's hard to know who to trust most of the time."

Nikolaus glanced at the counter where Valentina was fixing their drinks. She kept looking at them over the espresso machine. "She is one of them, but she doesn't know we know that yet. She thinks we still believe she is a supporter, like us. But we found out three weeks ago she has been relaying information to the other side."

Dana's mouth dropped. "What're you going to do?"

"We'll deal with her, but not yet. She still has her uses for now."

"Is she going to tell them I'm here?" Dana's concern was growing. If the Alaeshans found out where she was, if they knew she had switched sides and that she had the key... she wasn't sure she wanted to know what they would do. What if Charles found out? What would he do to Edith? What would Edith think?

"She might. But she doesn't yet know who you are. Most people don't. You're just two young American lovers who joined the fight."

Dana looked at the Chileans. "But we're not—"

"Here are your drinks." Dana jumped as Valentina appeared beside her with a tray and two drinks on top of it.

Aidan grinned at the young woman. "Thanks. You're a doll."

Valentina lowered her eyes coyly. "Not in front of your girlfriend," she playfully reprimanded, but the look on her face made it clear that she really didn't care if Dana was there or was his girlfriend.

The barista dropped off the drinks and went back to the counter to take the order of a man who had walked in.

Gisella raised her own mug to her lips. "Please try not to blow your cover, Aidan," she said over the rim before taking a sip of the steaming liquid.

"Ah, just having a bit of fun," he said.

"Yes, but you're supposed to be in love with Dana, remember?"

Aidan tossed Dana a wink. "Oh yes, I absolutely remember. And I am head over heels for the girl."

Dana blushed and coughed as she sipped her drink. "This is sweet," she said, trying to change the subject.

"Do you like it?"

Dana nodded at Gisella. "Yes. It's very good."

"I'm glad. Finish up. Once you're done, we will head to our house. We need to discuss some things. In private." The other woman's dark eyes shot to the counter once more where Valentina stood wiping down a glass and casting surreptitious glances their way.

A little while later, the group left the cafe and walked at a leisurely pace down the street. Elva, Dana, and Aidan played the part of tourists visiting family. Gisella and Nikolaus played the gracious hosts. For a time, Dana almost forgot that she was there on a very dire mission and lost herself in the beauty of the place. The architecture was stunning and the glimpses of mountain through the buildings left her breathless.

"This place is amazing," she said as they turned the corner to walk down another street. "These houses are incredible."

Gisella smiled. "Gracias. This is one of the nicer parts of Santiago, I'll admit. Niko and I were lucky to find such an affordable place here."

"You live here?"

The dark-haired woman nodded. "Just up there. Do you see the bright blue railing?"

Dana looked where Gisella was pointing. A lovely muted green townhouse popped with bright electric blue window railings, door, and other accents. Window boxes were filled with blooms all the colors of the rainbow. It was smushed between a bright pink home on one side and a canary yellow on the other. The girl couldn't help but grin.

"That's yours?"

"It is."

"You're so lucky. I wish houses were painted like this in the US."

Gisella laughed. "You should start a trend."

Dana's smile faded a bit. Her father would never, ever allow her to paint their house anything other than the basic middle-of-the-road tan that all the other houses in the suburb were.

Nikolaus unlocked the door and shepherded them all inside. Dana was even more impressed with the eclectic interior. It was bright and full of interesting stuff, but she barely had time to look at any of it as she was led to a sitting room. She settled onto a soft, teal love seat next to Aidan as she accepted the glass of lemonade offered by Gisella.

"Have you heard from Edith?" the woman asked Elva as she set the tray on the table and took a seat on a burnt orange chair.

"No, not yet. I fear for her. I've heard rumors that she was at a camp in the north."

"Yes, I have heard that as well. They took Gereld Anar."

Elva nodded. "Terrible news. What about his daughter?"

Gisella shook her head. "More rumors. Some that she was slaughtered. Others that she was captured. No one has any solid information."

Elva pressed her lips together. "That's unfortunate."

Dana frowned. "Edith wouldn't do that, would she? Kill a little girl?" She couldn't imagine her friend doing anything so horrible, but she hadn't seen Edith in months. Could she really have become that cruel?

Elva shrugged. "Before, I would say no. But we don't know what Charles has done to her, what he has convinced her of."

"We need to get through that door," Dana said more to herself than the others. She needed to find Edith. She needed to tell her the truth about what was going on, about who the Reformers really were. And most of all, she needed to know that Edith hadn't become a vicious murderer. She had to hang on to the hope that her friend was still the kind, strong girl she had known all summer.

They all agreed with her. "So how do we do that?"

Gisella cleared her throat and looked at Elva once more. "Does she know?"

Elva shook her head. "No. I haven't told her."

Dana's eyes narrowed. "Told me what?"

No one spoke. She poked Aidan with her elbow. "Told me what?" she repeated.

He cleared his throat and looked to Elva. The woman nodded. He shifted in his seat so he was able to look at Dana better. "There's a reason we brought you down here."

"Yeah, so I could help find a way to open the door."

His head bobbed side to side. "Sort of. We kind of already know how to open the door."

Dana's mouth dropped. "What? Why didn't you tell me?" Before she knew what she was doing, her fist snaked out and slammed into Aidan's arm.

"Ow. You do that a lot," he mumbled as he rubbed the sort spot.

"Sorry. It's kind of a default reaction. Why aren't we going through the doors if we know how to open them?"

Gisella sat forward. "Because we needed you to get through."

"Me?"

The woman nodded. "Yes. You. Dana, you're the piece we've been missing."

Dana shook her head. "No. That doesn't make any sense. I have nothing to do with the Fourth Door."

Gisella glanced at Nikolaus, then Elva. Elva folded her hands in her lap. "Dana," she said. "I haven't been completely truthful with you. The reason I brought you down here is because we've seen it. We've seen you go through the door."

"That doesn't make any sense. I can't get through the door unless someone else opens it."

"You have the key."

"It's not the right key. You can't just use any key on any door. That's not the way it works."

"We've seen it, Dana."

"Who's we? Who's seen it?"

Nikolaus rose and walked to the window. "My mother."

"And who, exactly, is she?"

"She's a seer."

"A seer? Like Tessa?"

Elva nodded. "Yes, but she's far less unstable. Her visions are reliable. Certain."

"And she saw me go through the door."

"Yes."

"How does she know I didn't go through after someone else opened it?"

Nikolaus turned from the window. "Because she saw you open it. You and you alone."

Dana looked around the room. All eyes were on her. She shifted uncomfortably in her seat. "So what are we waiting for?"

CHAPTER SIXTEEN

"It's not time," Gisella said.

Dana raised her eyebrows. "What does that even mean? If I can open the door, I should just go open the door. Why are we waiting?"

"We need to prepare before you go through. We need to be ready for anything."

"But Elva said the Reformers had the door on the other side. Why are we worried? Why can't we just go through and say 'Hey guys, we're here!'? What's the matter?"

Nikolaus sat down again. "There's still a war on that side. It's a fierce battle for the door. It might not be safe. We can't go through unprepared or we risk stumbling into the middle of something very bad."

Dana's excitement began to wither. "I'm not any good in battle."

Aidan patted her knee. "You don't have to be. I'll be there to protect you. And there are others who are trained for just this sort of thing. You'll have a guard. You'll be safe."

"A guard?"

Niko nodded. "Yes. Lejandra is in charge of the guard detail that will be assigned to you. She has picked a dozen of her best people. They will keep you protected on the other side."

"Only a dozen people are going through? I thought we're opening the door so we can move freely between the two worlds."

"Eventually that is the plan, but for now, we need to win this war. Once you get the door open, we can support the Reformers from this side."

Dana frowned. "How? What help are a bunch of humans going to be in a war against the Alaeshans? They have magic and stuff."

"There are many Reformers on this side, most who were banned from Alaesha for various reasons. And some who were trapped over here when the doors closed."

Dana's frown deepened. She wasn't sure how she felt about letting a bunch of people who had been kicked out of Alaesha back in. She also wasn't sure she wanted to be around those people. How bad do you have to be to get booted from an entire world? "Do we really want to be around people that have been banned from Alaesha? What'd they do? What if they're murderers?"

Nikolaus laughed a bit. "They're not. People are only banned for political reasons. They made the wrong people mad, took the wrong sides in a verbal conflict. Stuff like that. Things the various councils couldn't legally kill someone for."

Gisella looked at her watch. "Lejandra should be here soon. Once you meet her, I think you'll feel safer."

Dana wasn't sure about that, but she nodded. Almost on cue, a knock sounded at the door. "There she is." Nikolaus rose and disappeared from the room. He returned with a woman in her mid-twenties. Her dark, curly hair was pulled back, but little ringlets sprang from her head in an unruly fashion. Her mouth was set in a tight line and the wrinkles between her eyebrows hinted that scowling was her favorite facial expression.

She eyed Dana with a look of utter contempt. "That's her?" The disbelief bled from her voice in a torrent.

Gisella gave her a stern look. "Yes. Dana, I want you to meet Lejandra."

Lejandra's nose curled. She didn't even give Dana a chance to say hello. "This isn't going to happen. I'm not

103

taking a princesa sin valor into Alaesha. She'll be dead two steps out the door."

Dana stood up and slammed her fists onto her hips. "Excuse me? I am not worthless, and I am definitely not a princess." She took a step toward Lejandra. "I've been through more than you can possibly imagine so don't you dare think you can judge me or decide anything for me." Her heart was thumping in her ears and her breath was coming hard, but Dana was so irritated, she felt like she could fly across the coffee table and beat the living daylights out of the mouthy woman.

A wry smile pulled at the corner of Lejandra's mouth. "She has some fire, I'll give her that." She raised her chin and looked down her nose at Dana, even though Dana was taller than her by several inches. "All right, princesa. I'll take you to Alaesha. If you think you can get through the door."

Dana narrowed her eyes. "Why don't you just worry about your job and let me worry about mine, okay?"

Lejandra snorted. "Luchadora," she said to Gisella.

The other woman shrugged. "You made her mad."

Lejandra eyed Dana again. She nodded thoughtfully. "Yes, I will take you. But first, I will train you. You must be ready for anything when we get to the other side. Their war is not like ours. It is open, brutal, violent. If the battle is at the door, you will need to protect yourself and not rely on us to keep you safe."

Dana raised an eyebrow. "But isn't that your job? Why do I need you if I can take care of myself?"

Lejandra's smirk returned. "Necio." She shook her head. To Gisella, she said, "Bring her to my house tonight. I will make her ready."

Gisella tipped her head in acknowledgment. Lejandra gave Dana one last once-over and left without being shown the door.

When she was gone, Dana sat back down and crossed her arms. A scowl sat heavily on her face. "I don't like her," she growled.

Aidan grinned. "You two are going to be a lethal pair. Whether it's for the bad guys or turning on each other, only time will tell."

Dana turned her glare on him. "Shut up."

He tipped his head toward her. "Yes, ma'am."

Gisella rose from her seat. "Let me show you to your rooms. You should get some rest before tonight."

A few hours later, Dana was rubbing sleep from her bleary eyes as she walked down the street next to Gisella. The others had stayed behind to make further plans with Nikolaus.

"It's just up here," Gisella said after they had been walking awhile.

Dana rubbed her face again. She had dug out her sneakers after she realized how much crap Lejandra would give her for showing up in a pair of sandals. They felt tight and restrictive on her feet and her toes ached to be free, but she wouldn't give the other woman the satisfaction of judging her again. At least, not for that.

Gisella knocked on a plain, brown door. As it cracked open, Lejandra's scowling face greeted them. "Bring her inside," she said to Gisella.

"I have legs," Dana spat. "I can bring myself inside."

A faint smile played across Gisella's lips as she led the younger woman into the dark interior. The house was loud and dirty. Music thumped from somewhere up above and in the kitchen off to the immediate right, the sink was full of dishes.

"Almost all of Lejandra's team live here," Gisella explained. "Those without family stay with Lejandra."

"They're slobs." Dana's nose curled and she poked her toe at a dirty shirt lying on the floor.

"We have more important things to worry about than menial tasks such as cleaning." Lejandra's eyes were narrowed to bare slits as she glared at Dana. Her chin lifted. "Besides, we have a maid that comes once a week to do the cleaning."

Dana snorted. "Has she been sick?"

Lejandra's glare hardened. "No. She was here two days ago."

Dana opened her mouth to make another smart comment, but Gisella elbowed her hard in the side. "Enough. You have other things to worry about. I will return in a couple hours to retrieve you." With that, she left Lejandra and Dana glaring at each other in the hallway.

"Come." Lejandra turned and walked up the stairs.

Dana followed. A pair of men not much older than she was eyed her from a room off to the side as she walked by. They were in the midst of a video game and were the source of the loudest noise.

Lejandra waited for her by a door on the second floor. "In here."

The interior of the room was padded. On one wall, a door stood open to reveal an array of weapons.

"Choose your weapon."

Dana walked over to the closet. It was full of knives, swords and sticks of various shapes and sizes. She ran her fingers over a few of them, but ultimately turned away. "Hand-to-hand," she said.

Lejandra raised an eyebrow. "Oh?"

Dana raised her chin and matched Lejandra's stance. "Yes. I took Muay Thai when I was in school."

Amusement danced through Lejandra's eyes, but she uncrossed her arms and walked forward into the middle of the room. "Show me what you know."

Twenty seconds later, Dana lay on her back in the middle of the floor.

Lejandra walked around her like a lion circling its pray. "That was pathetic. Is that all you have?"

Embarrassment burned on Dana's face. Against many others, she was strong and confident, but this woman made her feel small and insignificant. Dana gritted her teeth. She wasn't weak. Her years of cheerleading had given her a toned body and she knew how to handle herself in combat. She bounced up to her feet. "Again."

The other woman smirked and lined herself up. The battle was a bit fiercer, but Dana still ended up in a pile on the ground. She popped up and lined herself up again. A half hour later, Lejandra hadn't lost a match, but she was breathing hard and had a bruise forming on her lower jaw.

"Enough," she said as she flattened Dana one more time.

Dana crawled to her feet. Her breath came short and her whole body ached, but she wasn't about to give up. She was going to take the warrior down. "No," she growled. "One more."

Lejandra shook her head. "We're done. You've shown me what you can do."

"I—"

"Stop. Take a compliment when you get it."

Dana placed her hands on her knees and bent over to catch her breath. She looked up at Lejandra. "That was a compliment?"

The other woman shrugged. "Close enough."

Dana snorted and shook her head. "You suck at compliments."

Lejandra smirked. "It's one of the few things I'm not good at."

"You're also very humble."

Lejandra's smirk held just a touch of honest smile. "You're not terrible. You should have kept up your lessons, but you have potential. Let's work with that."

By the time Gisella showed up, both women were exhausted, but Dana had taken Lejandra down twice and the dark-haired woman had a modicum of respect for the tough cheerleader.

"How'd it go?" Gisella stood in the door to the training room. Lejandra and Dana lounged on the floor, sucking down bottles of water.

Lejandra shrugged. "She'll do."

Gisella smiled. "I knew she would."

"What did you figure out?"

"We're going to have a block party. The restaurant and cafe will put out chairs and tables, offer up free snacks and drinks. There will be a ton of people. Few should notice when you go through the door."

"When is this happening?" Dana asked.

"Tomorrow."

Dana's mouth dropped. "How are you going to set up a block party in a day?"

"It'll be a spontaneous thing. A pop up party. They're very big right now. We have enough people in our support group that the news will spread like wildfire on social media."

"And you think that'll be enough to get a crowd to cover our going through the door?"

"It'll be plenty."

"So we go tomorrow." Dana looked down at her hands. They were shaking. She clenched them together. She was utterly terrified. In less than a day, she'd be walking into Alaesha, into who knew what. They had said the door was in the middle of a battlefield. Who owned it? The Reformers or the Alaeshans? Would they be killed instantly? Or welcomed with open arms? That's even if they made it through the door. Everyone was acting like they would, but what if the same thing happened that happened with the Third door? There was a good possibility the Fourth door wouldn't open at all, and if it did, that it wouldn't let them through the other side. Dana gritted her teeth together and did her best to hide her fears. Everyone else was so confident. She didn't want to be the weak link.

Lejandra got to her feet. "Go home. Get some sleep. You're going to need it." She gave Dana one last nod and disappeared out the door.

Dana was so tired, she barely made it back to Gisella's and dropped into her bed before she was sound asleep.

CHAPTER SEVENTEEN

Jilda poked at the eggs on her plate. Her cheek rested in her little hand and she pouted at her food.

Edith felt what the little girl was expressing, but she tried to hide it from Jilda. "What's the matter?" she asked as she sipped her coffee. "Don't like the eggs?"

"I want to see Papa. When can I see him again?" When she looked up, tears glistened at the corners of her eyes.

The little girl's pain ate at Edith's heart. She felt a lot of what Jilda felt. Both of them had suffered a lot in recent times. Edith had lost her entire world, and Jilda had basically done the same. Edith didn't want to talk to Charles. She didn't want to see him at all. But she couldn't take away Jilda's hope. "I don't know, little one. I'll talk to Charles today and ask if he'll let you see him."

Jilda returned to poking at her food, but her pout didn't disappear.

Later that day, Edith arranged for her and Jilda to meet Charles and Mags on the patio for a brief lunch. She had practically begged Mags to stay with them so she wasn't left alone with Charles. She didn't think she could handle that. The meal was awkward and uncomfortable, buoyed only by Mags's constant chatting. Once they were done eating, Edith cleared her throat and addressed Charles. "Can I talk to you a moment, please?"

He glanced at the door, but nodded. They moved out of earshot of the little girl.

"Jilda really wants to see her father," Edith said. She did her best to keep her voice even and keep any emotion out of it. She was still angry with Charles for his behavior regarding the girl, but he was the one standing between the child and her father. She needed his consent to let them see each other.

Charles shook his head immediately. "I can't allow that."

"What if I take her down? She'll be safe with me."

"No. It's not going to happen. You wanted her out of the dungeon and she's out. That's all I can do. I can't let her down there to see him." He crossed his arms and stared at her down his nose, silently daring her to test him.

Edith growled low in her throat and thought for a minute. "Let me see him, then. So I can tell her that he's doing okay."

"Just lie to her. Tell her you did. She's a kid. She'll believe you."

"Charles! What has gotten into you?" Edith's glare could skin a cat.

Charles sighed. "Fine. Have Mags watch her for a little bit right now. You can go down and talk to him for a minute. Just you. Not the girl."

Edith gave him a small smile. "Thank you. She'll appreciate that."

His mouth was twisted in annoyance. "Yeah, I hope she's not the only one." After he said it, his face fell. "I'm sorry. That was rude."

Edith didn't disagree. She kept her mouth shut so she didn't say anything that would get her banned from the dungeon. An awkward silence hung between them for a few moments while Charles shifted in his spot. Then he cleared his throat.

"Well, I have to go take care of some stuff." He waited a minute. Edith didn't respond. "Okay, um, bye." He gave her a nod.

"Bye," she said. Her heart twinged a little bit as he walked away, but she was still irritated with him about their earlier argument.

After he was gone, she asked Mags if she could take care of Jilda for a few minutes. Mags raised her eyebrows but agreed without prying any further.

Edith knelt in front of Jilda. "I'll be right back, okay? Be a good girl for Mags."

"I will." The little girl threw her arms around Edith in the biggest hug she could muster.

Edith put a smile on her face and waved as she walked into the house. It didn't take her long to find the nondescript door that led to the dungeon. It was as creepy and horrid as she remembered and the stench threatened to overpower her.

"Can I help you, Miss Edith?" A guard met her at the bottom of the stairs. His hand rested lightly on the sword at his waist, a subtle reminder that this was his domain and would tolerate no funny business.

"I'm here to see Gereld."

He raised his eyebrows and shrugged. "Don't know no one by that name."

Edith rolled her eyes. "The scientist?"

"Ah, yes. He's not allowed any visitors."

"Charles said I could speak to him for a few minutes."

The man's mouth pressed into a line. He stared at her for a full thirty seconds. "Okay, but just a few minutes. Not a minute longer."

He stepped aside and let her by. He followed her down the hall of cells until she was standing in front of Gereld's door. "Can you open it?" She waved a hand at the cell.

"No. That is one thing I will not do. Talk through the bars."

"Can we at least have a little privacy?"

"No." He tilted his chin up and set his hand more firmly on the hilt of his sword.

Edith glared at him, but it didn't do any good.

111

"Jilda?" A soft call came from inside the cell. "Is that my daughter?" Gereld's face appeared at the bars. A long, bleeding cut trailed down the side of his face. His nose was clearly broken and a bruise purpled his chin.

"No, it's me, Edith. I'm taking care of your daughter."

"Edith. You're the one that saved her from this place."

A small blush crept into Edith's cheeks, but she nodded. "Yes."

"How is she?"

"She's doing okay. She misses you."

A sad smile played across Gereld's lips. "And I her."

"Are you okay?"

He shrugged. "As to be expected. This is war. Nothing is sacred anymore."

An oppressing sadness settled into Edith's heart. Gereld had given up. It was clear from his tone and words. "Your daughter is. She's a very sweet child. She doesn't deserve to be a part of this war."

Gereld closed his eyes a moment and nodded. "Yes, she is. She is more special than you know. Take care of her, Edith. Please. Protect her and love her as your own. She is bright and will give you the world if you only give it back to her."

Tears sprang to Edith's eyes. "I will. I promise."

He put his hands up to the bars. Edith reached up and gently touched his swollen fingers. They exchanged a small smile. Gereld gave her a brief nod and disappeared from the window.

Edith stood there a moment until the guard urged her away. A sadness formed a knot in the pit of her stomach as she walked up the stairs. She had a horrible feeling that she would never see Gereld again.

An hour later, she was out on the patio with Jilda. They had draw a hopscotch grid on the stones with some chalk and Edith was teaching the little girl how to play. Edith picked up the pebble they were using in place of a bean bag and tossed it further down the board.

"Hop, hop," Jilda called.

Edith picked up one leg and bounced forward. The ground moved beneath her feet and she almost fell over. The whole house rocked. The glasses on the table rattled and the pebble skittered across the stones.

Jilda's wide eyes found Edith. The young woman dropped to her knees and held out her arms. She enclosed the little girl in them and held her tight.

A minute later, Mags appeared at the door. "To your room. Quickly. Lock yourselves in. Go now."

Edith took Jilda's hand and they raced into the house and up the stairs. Shouts echoed from various parts of the house. Edith slammed the door behind them and locked it tight. Jilda stood beside her. Her wide eyes swam with tears that poured over and streamed down her cheeks.

"What's wrong, Edith?"

Edith took Jilda's hand and led her to the bed. "I don't know, sweetheart. I don't know. Stay here, okay?"

Jilda climbed onto the bed and grabbed her doll. She held it tight as Edith walked across the room and pressed her ear to the door. She heard nothing. She walked to the window and looked out. Again, nothing. No more quakes rocked the house. All was silent. Eerily so.

After a few minutes, she opened the armoire along the wall and turned on a cartoon for Jilda. They were watching a funny-looking creature dance across the screen when a knock came at the door.

Edith stood and walked across the floor.

"Open the door, Edith," a call came from outside. It wasn't Charles voice. It was a woman. Boxy.

Edith inhaled and steeled herself. Something bad had happened. She almost didn't want to know what it was.

She opened the door. Charles stood beside Boxy. Their faces were lined with anger. Boxy's hand was raised to knock again. When the door swung open, she slammed her fist into the door frame. "Where's the girl?" she demanded.

Edith stepped into the hall and pulled the door shut behind her. "She's in there, watching television. What happened? What's wrong?"

Boxy's nostrils flared. If she was a dragon, she would've burned the whole house down. "Your Reformer pet blew himself up," she hissed.

"What? How?"

Charles was a little more composed than Boxy, but not by much. "He's a scientist. He knows magic better than all of us. Somehow, he created a bomb. When Veth went to question him, he blew it. Killed one of my guards and wounded Veth."

Edith's jaw dropped as her heart sank into her gut. "Veth?" she whispered. She pressed her hand to her chest. Veth was one of the kindest people in Alaesha. He was always full of laughter and a smile for Edith. She thought Gereld was a good guy, misunderstood in his cause but still good. Now she wasn't sure anymore. She was still trying to wrap her head around the news when Boxy stepped up until she was toe-to-toe with her.

"I want the girl." Boxy's snarl was so venomous, Edith was actually afraid of her. But Edith wasn't about to let anyone have the child. She had made a promise she intended to keep.

Edith's concern for Veth was still strong, but she raised her chin and crossed her arms. "No." She wasn't about to let a four-year-old child pay for something the girl's father had decided to do. This war wasn't Jilda's fault and she wasn't going to suffer for it just because Boxy had anger issues.

Boxy growled and stepped closer. Her breath was hot on Edith's face. "Give me... the girl."

Fear crept up Edith's spine. She had seen what Boxy was capable of, but something inside her was stronger than the fear. She straightened and looked Boxy straight in the eyes. "No freaking way."

Boxy shouted and slammed her fist into the wall. "Charles, bring your human to heel."

Charles snorted. "She's not 'my human'. She's my girlfriend. And this is your battle with her, not mine."

Edith glanced at Charles. She didn't know how to react to that. First off, he had called her his girlfriend, so at least they were still together, even if they weren't seeing eye-to-eye at the moment. Second, he refused to take Boxy's side. That was another small plus in his direction. Maybe he was starting to come around. Then again, he hadn't taken her side either. Maybe he was waiting to see who would win.

Boxy pointed at the door. If she were an animal, her fangs would be dripping. The venom in her voice was enough to burn holes in Charles's head. "That child is a Reformer. She is the daughter of the scientist who just killed people in *your* basement. Her father nearly killed one of your best friends. And you're going to let this..." The utter contempt on her face threatened to crumple Edith's resolve. "This girl overrule you in your own home?"

Charles own face grew hard. "First off, you have no right to speak to me that way. As you said, this is *my* home. Not yours. You are a guest here. Second, this is Edith's home too. And she is in charge of the child. The girl is hers to do with as she will. You will not make the decision for her, or for me. The child may be born of Reformers, but she is not one herself until she makes the decision. For now, she is an orphan under my protection and Edith's care. You will not threaten her. You will not hurt her. You will not punish her for her father's crimes. She is not part of this."

Edith's heart soared. Charles *was* taking her side. Was he finally coming around to see that Jilda was just a child, no more Reformer or Alaeshan than the animals that milled about in the yard? Did he finally get it?

Boxy's anger let off a palpable heat. Edith wanted to cower in a corner before her, but Charles stood between them and refused to back down. Edith felt like she was witnessing something incredible, two guardians of enormous power in a stand-off on opposite sides of the battlefield.

Boxy snarled at Charles, but she looked around him to speak to Edith. "This isn't over, girl. You are harboring the enemy. When the child turns on you, you will be looking for us to have your back, and I for one will not be there." She glared at Charles. "You're a fool," she spat before she turned away and stormed down the stairs.

Edith and Charles watched her go. When they heard the door leading outside slam shut, Edith turned to Charles. "Thank you," she said. "Thank you so much."

Anger mingled with a strange sadness on his face. "Please do not make me regret this, Edith. You have no idea what I've just done, how much I've put myself on the line for this."

Edith shook her head. "You won't. Charles, she's a kid. And now that her father is gone, she has no one. We're it. We can't just turn her over to be tortured for no reason. You're not that kind of person."

Charles looked like he was going to be sick. "I don't know what kind of person I am, anymore, Edith. I really don't."

She laid a hand on his arm. It was the first time she had touched him in... she couldn't remember the last time. "You're a good man, Charles. I know you are. You can be the person I fell in love with." She didn't know why she said that, but she truly felt it. Her anger with him for his behavior surrounding Jilda faded. That wasn't him. That was him letting others rule his thoughts. No, it wasn't Charles. The Charles she knew regretted what he had done to the child. That regret sat heavy on his face.

"I hope you're right. I want to do the right thing, but I don't know what that is anymore."

Edith squeezed his arm gently. "I know. I know how you feel. There are very few things I'm certain of anymore. But Jilda is one."

They were both silent for a few minutes, just standing there next to each other. It was the most they had been together without fighting in a long time.

Charles sighed. "I have a lot to think about." He reached up and touched her cheek. "I love you, Edith," he said before walking away.

116

CHAPTER EIGHTEEN

The party was in full swing when Dana, Elva, and Aidan arrived at the cafe. Street vendors had been invited to set up their wares, the road had been blocked, and the restaurant was doling out free snacks. A juggler did somersaults while tossing brightly colored balls in the air. A unicyclist danced between the spectators on his enormous wheel.

"This is insane," Dana breathed. "How are we ever going to find anyone?"

"They're already in the cafe." Gisella led the way through the crowd.

Sure enough, Lejandra and a couple of her crew were camped out in the cafe at a handful of tables. She stood up as soon as they entered. "Here," she said, holding out a paper cup to Dana. "Let's go."

Dana's eyes went wide. "Already? Don't we get to hang out and enjoy the festivities for a few minutes?"

Lejandra glared at her. "Are you backing out?"

Dana shuffled her feet. "No, I just—"

"Good. Let's go." Lejandra picked up a long duffel bag that had been stuffed under the table and threw it over her shoulder. She walked outside and let out a sharp whistle. Everyone nearby turned to stare at her, but she ignored them and walked toward the restaurant.

"The door is that way," Dana said, pointing in the other direction as she raced to catch up to Lejandra.

The woman stared at her. "I just drew a ton of attention to myself. Would you like us to head to the door right now so everyone knows what we're doing?"

Dana shuffled beside her. "No, I guess not."

Aidan caught up to them. "So what's the plan?"

Lejandra stopped in front of a light pole and leaned against it. She pulled out a cigarette. As she lit it, she gave them the low-down. "We meet in front of the door. Dana opens it. We go through."

Aidan laughed. "Simple."

"Exactly." She took a puff and blew it out. They stood in silence as she finished her cigarette. "Let's go." She pushed herself away from the pole and led the way across the street.

When they reached the Fourth Door, a small crowd was gathered in front. Off to the left, the juggler pulled out six torches and lit them all. As he began his act, nearly everyone turned to watch.

"Open the door," Lejandra said.

Dana looked around. The only people in the nearby vicinity not looking at the juggler were Lejandra's crew. She glanced at Aidan. He gave her an encouraging smile and a nod. She took a deep breath and pulled out the key. As she walked toward the door, her stomach began to match the flips of the juggler. She moved the key toward the lock. It slid in. A collective gasp went up from the crowd. Dana spun. They weren't looking at her. The juggler had one of the torches, flame side down, in his mouth. Everyone began to clap. Dana turned back. She turned the key. The lock clicked. Her heart fluttered.

"Open it. Hurry." Aidan was right next to her. Lejandra stood nearby, at full alert. Her hand was tight on the duffel bag handle. Her crew had arrayed themselves in a semi-circle, blocking the door from view.

Dana swung the door open. A small light clicked on, but it revealed little aside from a Welcome mat just inside the foyer.

"Go." Lejandra pushed Dana through the doorway. Aidan followed. In a few moments, the whole dozen were inside.

Dana looked around. It looked just like the interior of a house. Stairs led up into blackness and a hallway led off away from the door. "Now what?"

"Take these."

She looked at the items Lejandra offered her. It was a pair of gloves, designed to protect your hands in a fight. Dana slipped them on. All around her, the others were pulling weapons of all sorts from the duffel bags they carried. Soon, they were armed to the teeth.

"Leave the bags here," Lejandra commanded. "Take only what we need."

Aidan had a pistol in one hand. Lejandra carried a sword. Another man, Rio, held a pair of nunchukas.

Lejandra led the way, followed by Rio and a couple others. Dana and Aidan were shuffled to the middle of the pack. They walked past the stairs, into the dark hallway beyond. As they moved forward, tiny lights on the walls lit up to show the way. They shut off after they had passed beyond their small circle of illumination.

The house didn't end where Dana expected it to. The hallway just kept going. She was used to the tunnel underneath the diner. That made sense to her. A tunnel was underground. But the hallway didn't droop and there were no stairs.

"How is this even possible?" she asked after they had walked a quarter of a mile in the hallway.

Aidan grinned at her. "Magic, my dear."

Dana ran her hand along the wallpaper and examined the carpet below her feet. "Magic," she repeated.

They walked on for another ten minutes until Lejandra held up her hand. "Down," she hissed. "Get down."

"What's going on?" Dana asked.

"Be quiet." Rio glared at Dana before facing front again.

A few second later, she heard something from up ahead. The hallway should have been dead silent, and yet there was obviously movement.

"I swear I heard something," came a voice from in the dark.

Lejandra looked back and pressed a finger to her lips. Dana's heart thumped so loud she was afraid they could hear it a mile away. She reached out and gripped Aidan's free hand. He gave her a brave smile, but his own face was pale and worried.

The sounds grew closer. Lejandra held her hand out toward her group, palm up. Then she rose to her feet and moved forward. "Who's there?" she called down the hallway.

The sounds stopped aside from a faint whisper that Dana couldn't hear.

Lejandra held up her sword. "Whoever you are, show yourself now."

Another minute of silence passed before someone stepped forward. It was a woman with bluish-green hair. She held her hands up, palms forward. A sign of peace.

"Who are you?" she asked Lejandra.

"No. Who are you? How'd you get in here?" Lejandra's sword tip pointed right at the woman's throat.

The woman eyed the group arrayed behind Lejandra. "I am Miria Anar."

Lejandra's sword drooped a bit. "The scientist's wife?"

A sad smile crossed the woman's face. "No, I am the scientist. My husband Gereld was good with magic, but he was not as advanced in science as I am. He did not understand it like I can."

Lejandra let the tip of her sword fall until it was pointed toward the ground. "You said 'was'. What happened?"

Miria's eyes got a far away look. "They found our camp. The Alaeshans. We were attacked. Gereld stayed behind to protect our daughter. I hid in the woods. They were both taken. I doubt either are still alive."

"I'm so sorry." Lejandra waved to the group. "Dana, come here."

Dana rose to her feet and moved forward. She kept herself just behind Lejandra. The other woman seemed to trust the stranger, but she didn't.

"Dana?" Miria asked. "The Keeper of the Third Key?"

"Former Keeper," Dana muttered, but then she remembered the key sitting in her pocket.

"How did you get in here without a key?" Miria addressed her question to Lejandra again. The dark haired woman was clearly in charge.

Lejandra paused a moment before turning halfway to the young woman behind her. "Dana?"

"Um, well." Dana ran a hand through her blond hair. "We went through the Third Door—"

"How?" Miria's eyes were narrowed as she looked at the girl.

Dana shrugged. "I dunno. It just opened. Let us through. But it wouldn't let us in on the other side. It wouldn't let us into Alaesha."

"So how did you get into this door?"

"Edith left the Third Key sitting in the other door. So I took it."

"You have a key?"

Dana nodded.

"Can I see it?"

Dana looked at Lejandra. The other woman bobbed her head. Dana removed the key from her pocket and held it out so Miria could see it. Miria's fingers hovered over the shiny metal, but she did not touch it.

"Thank you," she said. "That key was left in the Third Door?"

"Yeah, on this side."

"And it let you back out?"

Dana nodded again.

"You used it to get into the Fourth Door?"

"Mmhmm."

Miria tapped her chin. "How interesting. I've never heard of that happening before. There is no mention of one key being used in another door. I wonder if this is a one-time occurrence or if it has never been tried."

Lejandra dismissed the second conjecture. "They tried the Seventh Key in the Fourth Door. It didn't work."

Miria eyed Dana up and down. "It must be something about you. It let you through for a reason."

"What reason?" Dana asked.

Miria shrugged. "I guess we'll find out." She looked at Lejandra's group. They had all risen to their feet by this point. "Come." She turned around and began to walk back down the hallway from the way she had come.

"Wait," Dana called. "Don't you want to go to my world?"

Miria stopped and looked at her. "The door let you through. It meant for you to come to Alaesha. I want to know why."

Dana's eyes darted between Lejandra and Aidan. "What do we do?" she asked.

Lejandra shrugged. "We follow."

"Do we trust her?"

"Do you?"

Dana stared down the hallway where Miria had disappeared. She took a deep breath. "Yes." She turned and followed Miria into the darkness. The rest of the group followed behind.

In no time at all, they reached the other door. Miria stood waiting for them. She gave Dana a smile. "Are you ready to see what we have accomplished so far?"

Dana glanced at Aidan. He moved up beside her and gave her a wink. Dana nodded.

Miria swung the door open. On the other side lay a steep incline that led down to a field filled with tents and moving bodies. The Reformer army writhed over the land. Something roared overhead and Dana ducked instinctively.

She spun and looked above the door. A dragon perched on the mountainside, its claws digging into the stone.

"Rayu," Miria said by way of explanation. "Guardian of the Fourth Door."

"Wait, what? You have a Guardian in the Reformers?"

"Yes. Not everyone is as foolish as those who refuse to change."

Dana stared at the dragon a moment longer before turning to look at the massive army laid out below her. Her skewed little view of Alaesha changed in an instant. She suddenly realized just how big this war was and what exactly she had gotten herself in to. Her hand found Aidan's and squeezed it tight.

CHAPTER NINETEEN

Edith was playing on the patio with Jilda when Mags came out to see them. No one had told the little girl what had happened to her father, that he now numbered among the ever rising casualties of the war. Edith didn't want to tell her until there was no other choice. Why break the little girl's heart if she didn't have to?

"Charles wants to see you." Mags gave Edith a smile. "I'll watch Jilda."

The joy Edith felt when she was playing with the little girl turned to apprehension. She hadn't seen him since the discussion after Gereld killed himself and almost took Veth with him. "Did he say what he wanted?"

"He's been doing a lot of thinking. We've spent the last three nights talking about everything, and he wants to talk to you and make it right."

Edith bit her lip. Her heart fluttered. She really hoped Mags was right. She loved Charles, but could they work it out? She hoped so. "Where is he?"

"In the garden."

Edith raised an eyebrow. The garden used to be a beautiful place until it was partly destroyed by the attack on the house. It was where they shared their first breakfast.

"By the waterfall." Mags gave her a knowing smile.

"They fixed it?"

"Somewhat."

Edith swallowed. He wanted to meet by the waterfall, a romantic little place that he knew she loved. "All right." She leaned over and gave Jilda a little peck on the forehead. "Behave for Mags, okay?"

Jilda bobbed her head. "I will. Mags, here's your dolly." She thrust one of the myriad of toys at Charles's older sister. Mags took it graciously and gave Edith a wink.

Edith watched them a moment before she headed into the house. She found her way to the garden and stepped inside. The glass ceiling was still under repair, but all the wreckage had been removed. The waterfall in the middle had sustained minimal damage and had already been fixed. She found Charles sitting at the table where they had first shared breakfast.

"Have a seat," he said as she walked into the clearing.

A small silver tray sat on the table with two glasses and a jar of bualdaberry tea. Charles poured the tea and handed her a cup. She took a sip and stared into the glass.

"I'm sorry," he said.

She glanced up.

"I'm sorry I turned you into a killer. When we first met, I didn't even think about what that would do to you. How it would make you feel. It's just such a part of me, who I am, what Alaesha is, that I didn't consider how it would impact you. I'm sorry I was so horrible about Jilda, too. You're absolutely right. She's an innocent child. She doesn't deserve to be blamed for the actions of her parents. She has absolutely nothing to do with them and she deserves a peaceful, happy life. And I'm sorry I made you feel like you weren't important, like all I cared about was this war. I do care about the war, and I can't stop fighting it, but I had almost forgotten the reason I was fighting."

He paused and she waited. Her stomach fluttered as he spoke. Was that really how he felt? She held her breath and dared to hope.

"You're the reason, Edith. Before I met you, I was doing it because I had to, because it was my job, what my family would expect. But then you came and everything changed. You became my reason, my only reason. I want to make this a safe, happy place for you to live."

Edith's eyes welled up with tears. "Oh, Charles." She reached across the table and took his hand. "It's not your fault. Not all of it. I didn't think I'd have such a hard time with the war. I didn't think it would affect me like it has. I'm sorry for not being honest with you from the beginning, for not telling you how hard things were for me. It didn't help either of us." She brushed his thumb. She wanted to broach the subject of whether he was on the right side of the war or not, but she wasn't sure how to bring it up.

Charles smiled and leaned across the table. He flipped his hand over, palm up. She placed her hand in his and he gripped it tight. "You don't have to be a part of this war if you don't want to be, Edith." He wasn't being mean. He was being honest. His smile faded. "You don't have to be in Alaesha either. I don't want you to leave, but if you want to, if you want to take Jilda and go back to your world, I'll find a way to get you home. I promise. Even if it means I have to talk to the Reformers at the Seventh Door. I don't want to make you stay here if you're not happy. I'll do whatever it takes to get you home."

Edith's mouth parted. She stared at him. The sadness and despair that sat heavily in his eyes broke her heart. He loved her, but he was willing to let her take Jilda and go if that's what she wanted. He would find a way to make it work, even if it meant going against everyone he knew to make it happen. "No, Charles. I don't want to go back. I just want to be with you, like we talked about before. I only want you."

His smile returned and he held her hand tighter. He breathed a sigh of relief. "I'm so glad you said that. I promise I'll try to do better. I may not be perfect and I'm sure I'll make lots of mistakes, but I'll try my best."

She returned his smile. "Me, too. I think if we both try, we can make it work."

"And Jilda has nothing to fear. She is safe in our protection. This is her home too, now. If anyone doesn't like that..." He shrugged. "They know where the door is."

126

Edith's heart soared, but a tingle of fear crept up her spine. "What if they disagree? What if they think you're harboring a Reformer?"

Charles shook his head. "I've thought about that a lot. I've thought about a lot of things, actually. Jilda isn't a Reformer. We're officially adopting her. Anyone who disagrees with that can deal with me."

Edith grinned. Tears stung her eyes, but unlike most of her tears lately, they were happy tears. She still wasn't sure whether they were on the right side of the war, but she decided that right now wasn't the time to bring that up. Charles was starting to question his own beliefs. He was putting his reputation on the line to adopt the daughter of a famous Reformer scientist. That was a huge step. She was okay with leaving it there for the time being. There would be plenty of time to deal with the other issues later. Jilda was safe. Edith no longer had to go into battle. And Boxy could stuff it if she didn't like any of it.

They sat in the mist of the waterfall holding hands for a few minutes. Then Charles looked up at Edith with a sly grin on his face. "I think we have the beginning of our family, whether you're ready for it or not."

Edith's eyes went wide, but her heart felt much lighter than it had in months. "That's a discussion for another time, I think."

He laughed and leaned over the table to give her a kiss. He stood up and led her out of the garden. They spent the rest of the day playing with Jilda and Mags on the patio, testing the waters as a family.

Thank you for reading the Fourth Key. If you enjoyed it, please consider leaving a review at your favorite bookseller.

Series By Samantha Warren

Blood of the Dragon – An Epic YA Fantasy

The Iron Locket – A Paranormal Romance

Massacre at Lonesome Ridge – A Zombie Western

Jane (The Vampire Assassin series) – An Urban Fantasy

Space Grease & Pixie Dust - A Sci-fi Steampunk Serial

The Alaesha Legacy – A YA Urban Fantasy

Zombie Juice (Coming Soon) – A NA Zombie Serial

About the Author

Samantha Warren is a speculative fiction author who spends her days immersed in dragons, spaceships, and vampires. She milks cows for fun, collects zombie gnomes, and dreams about the day she'll meet Boba Fett. Her love is easily purchased with socks and her goal in life is to eat a Beef Wellington cooked by Gordon Ramsay.

Interested in contacting Samantha?
Email: samantha@samantha-warren.com
Twitter: @_SamanthaWarren
Blog: http://www.samantha-warren.com
Facebook:
http://www.facebook.com/AuthorSamanthaWarren

www.ingramcontent.com/pod-product-compliance
Lightning Source LLC
Chambersburg PA
CBHW060353180626
46817CB00008B/3000